Love

BIG SKY CENTENNIAL

HER MONTANA TWINS
Carolyne Aarsen

D0052015

HER MONTANA TWINS
Big Sky Centennial
Carolyne Aarsen

HER HOMETOWN HERO
Caring Canines
Margaret Daley

SMALL-TOWN BILLIONAIRE
Renee Andrews

THE DEPUTY'S NEW FAMILY
Jenna Mindel

**STRANDED WITH
THE RANCHER**
Tina Radcliffe

**RESCUING THE
TEXAN'S HEART**
Mindy Obenhaus

ISBN-13: 978-0-373-87907-6

50599

 EAN

Ladies and Gentlemen, start your bidding!
The Jasper Gulch Centennial Committee
Proudly Presents
The Jasper Gulch Fall Fair
and Picnic Basket Auction

Who needs speed dating and online matchmaking? Jasper Gulch believes in doing things the old-fashioned way. And what could be sweeter than an old-time picnic basket auction? As the town's potential suitors line up to place their bids, no one is more excited than auction coordinator Hannah Douglas. Of course, the young widow has no interest in finding a date—or so she says.

But this centennial celebrating is having a strange effect on *everyone,* and nothing is as it seems. The time capsule is still missing, there have been unexplained events and someone has even convinced the town pastor to make a basket! With all the unusual goings-on in town, anything is possible. Even a sweet single mom finding love a second time around....

* * *

Big Sky Centennial:
A small town rich in history...and love.

Her Montana Cowboy by Valerie Hansen—*July 2014*
His Montana Sweetheart by Ruth Logan Herne—*August 2014*
Her Montana Twins by Carolyne Aarsen—*September 2014*
His Montana Bride by Brenda Minton—*October 2014*
His Montana Homecoming by Jenna Mindel—*November 2014*
Her Montana Christmas by Arlene James—*December 2014*

Books by Carolyne Aarsen

Love Inspired

CAROLYNE AARSEN

and her husband, Richard, live on a small ranch in northern Alberta, where they have raised four children and numerous foster children, and are still raising cattle. Carolyne crafts her stories in an office with a large west-facing window, through which she can watch the changing seasons while struggling to make her words obey.

Her Montana Twins
Carolyne Aarsen

Special thanks and acknowledgment to Carolyne Aarsen for her contribution to the Big Sky Centennial miniseries.

Recycling programs
for this product may
not exist in your area.

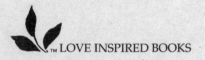

™ LOVE INSPIRED BOOKS

ISBN-13: 978-0-373-87907-6

HER MONTANA TWINS

www.Harlequin.com

Printed in U.S.A.

God is our refuge and strength.
An ever present help in trouble. Therefore we
will not fear though the earth give way and the
mountains fall into the heart of the sea.
—*Psalms* 46:1–2

To my agent, Karen Solem—thanks for your work,
for your support and encouragement through
all the ups and downs of this crazy writing life.

Chapter One

"**I** tell you it was rigged." Lilibeth Shoemaker tucked her cell phone in the back pocket of her snug blue jeans and rested her elbows on the waist-high wooden counter separating Hannah's desk from the large open waiting area of the town hall. Light from the mullioned window above the large double doors created a halo out of Lilibeth's blond hair. However, the effect was negated by narrowed blue eyes enhanced by dark eyeliner and pouting red lips. "There is no way Alanna Freeson should have won that and not me." This last word was emphasized with a slap of the hand on the divider.

Hannah Douglas gave Lilibeth what she called her Customer Care smile while she typed a quick note on the application for a booth for the county fair Hannah was helping to organize. This year the fair was to be the biggest ever in honor of Jasper Gulch's hundredth anniversary and Hannah was already behind. All morning she'd been fighting a headache, juggling her attention between her increasing workload and her concerns over her mother, who was babysitting Hannah's twins. This morning her mother had shown up looking drawn and pale but, as usual, insisting everything was fine.

Lilibeth tapped a long zebra-striped fingernail on the counter as if to get Hannah's attention. "I was told I had to talk to you about it."

Hannah hit Enter, then turned her chair to devote her entire attention to Lilibeth. The young girl had flounced into the town hall a few minutes ago exuding an air of long suffering that Hannah knew masked a simmering frustration with losing the Miss Jasper Gulch contest. Though the winner had been crowned at the Fourth of July picnic, launching the town's centennial festivities two months ago now, Lilibeth had complained loudly since then to anyone who would listen that she had been robbed. She was determined to get to the bottom of whatever conspiracy she seemed to think had been hatched.

"There's nothing I can do," Hannah said. "The contest is over and the winner has been determined."

As she reasoned with Lilibeth, the heavy doors of the town hall office opened and a tall figure stepped inside the foyer. Though the entrance of the converted bank building boasted ten-foot-high ceilings, Brody Harcourt easily dominated the space and Hannah's attention.

He stood in the doorway now, his eyes skimming the interior as he swept his cowboy hat off his dark hair. The sleeves of his shirt were rolled up over muscular forearms and his ramrod-straight stance bespoke his firefighter training, but the sprinkle of straw on his brown cowboy hat probably came from working on the ranch he and his father owned. He glanced at the empty chairs lining one wall, interspersed with potted plants, but stayed standing.

"But you take minutes at the town council meetings, dontcha? Couldn't you find out stuff for me?" Lilibeth's question was underlined with a nervous tap, tap of her fingernail. As Hannah's attention was drawn back to the young girl, she fought a yawn.

Chrissy, her thirteen-month-old daughter, was cutting teeth and she'd been up most of the night crying and feverish. Thankfully, her twin brother, Corey, had slept through all of the fussing. Unfortunately, Hannah had not. She'd spent most of the evening rocking Chrissy and walking the floor with her hoping her cries wouldn't wake Miss Abigail Rose, who lived in the apartment beside Hannah's above the hardware store. Miss Rose had been reluctant to continue subletting the adjoining apartment to Hannah precisely because of the twins. She had given in when Hannah's mother had shamed Miss Rose by saying this was no way to treat the widow of a soldier who'd died for his country. Hannah knew she was only staying at the apartment on sufferance, widow or not, and as a result was hyperconscious of any noise the babies made.

"I'm taking care of organizing the fair this year and the picnic basket auction," Hannah said. "I can help you if you want to donate a basket or if you want a booth at the fair. Unfortunately, I can't do anything about the Miss Jasper Gulch contest and neither can Mayor Shaw."

Lilibeth pursed her lips, winding a strand of hair around her finger as she contemplated this information. "So you can't get hold of the minutes of the meetings or stuff and let me see them? I need to find out if this was a setup or not."

Why was she so intent on digging so deeply into this?

A movement from Brody distracted Hannah from Lilibeth's questions. He was glancing at his watch, as if checking the time. Then he looked over at her, angled her a quick smile and raised his eyebrows toward

Lilibeth, as if he was sympathizing with Hannah having to deal with the young lady's self-indulgent antics.

"The contest was run separately from town business." Hannah kept her smile intact as she turned her attention back to Lilibeth. "And even if the council was involved, I wouldn't be at liberty to give you the minutes of the meetings."

As Hannah spoke, Robin Frazier entered the foyer from the office she and Olivia Franklin worked in. She clutched a sheaf of papers and had a pencil behind one ear holding her blond hair back from her face. Probably seeking more information for the genealogy study she had come to Jasper Gulch for. She and Olivia had been working together on the history of the town as part of her studies.

"Are you going to donate a basket for the auction?" Hannah asked Lilibeth, trying to distract the girl and hurry her on.

Lilibeth gave Hannah a confused look as if not certain of this sudden switch in the conversation. "I'm not sure I could organize a basket. What would I put in it?"

"Food. Snacks. Treats. Sandwiches. Be creative," Hannah said, handing her a paper. "Here's a submission form to fill out. We're doing something different this year. Instead of just food baskets, we are asking for some people to consider making a themed basket instead."

"Themed basket?"

"Yes. You could make a basket of books. A basket of bath products. Snack foods. Baby stuff. The form will give you some ideas. You can choose which one you prefer." While the young woman puzzled over the paper, Hannah turned her attention to Brody.

"Can I help you, Mr. Harcourt?"

Brody Harcourt gave her an affronted look as he came to the counter. "Whoa, what's with the mister? I'm twenty-nine. That's only four years older than you."

In a town the size of Jasper Gulch, anyone who was four years older than you in high school seemed to stay in that exalted position until you got to know them. And Brody moved in different circles than she did, so she never got to know him well.

"Sorry. Just trying to be respectful of the age difference." Hannah didn't know where that little quip came from, but the twinkle in Brody's eye and the way his mouth curved upward in a half smile created a curious uptick in her heartbeat. He really was quite attractive.

And still single, which surprised her. She thought someone like Brody would have been snatched up years ago.

"Glad to know I get some respect around here," he said, setting his hat on the wide counter between them.

Lilibeth looked up from the form she still held. The frown puckering her forehead shifted in an instant, and her smile made a blazing reappearance.

"Hey, there, Brody," she almost purred. "How are things at the Harcourt ranch?"

"Fall's coming, so it's busy," Brody said, giving the young girl a grin.

"You going to enter in the demolition derby going on in Bozeman this year?"

"Don't have a vehicle to enter and I don't have time."

"You did real well the last time you entered," Lilibeth continued, laying her hand lightly on his arm in a distinctly flirtatious gesture. "Couldn't believe how you smashed up the competition. Fearless. Living up to your nickname, Book-it Brody."

Hannah knew Brody's high school nickname had

less to do with academics than it had with his penchant for driving fast trucks and outrunning the sheriff of the day. Though that was in his past, he still held a reputation for being a risk-taker, not the kind of person Hannah could allow herself, a widowed mother of two, to be attracted to. The admiration in Lilibeth's voice at Brody's apparent recklessness only underlined Hannah's previous assessment of Brody Harcourt.

In spite of that, when he turned back to her and his smile deepened, she was unable to look away from his dark gaze.

Again Hannah pushed down her foolish reaction, not sure what was wrong with her these days. It seemed that she'd had romance on her mind lately. She wanted to blame it on her friend Julie's recent engagement or the plans for the Old Tyme wedding coming up next month, but the truth was, she'd been feeling lonely the past few months. The first year after David's death, she had been on autopilot, trying to absorb the reality that her husband of only a couple of months was killed so soon after shipping out to Afghanistan. She had often felt that their brief marriage was an illusion, even though the twins that came of that marriage certainly weren't.

"I understand you're the person I need to talk to about reserving a booth at the fair?" Brody said, resting his elbows on the counter and leaning closer. "It's for the firefighters."

"I'll get the form you need," she said as the door of the hall opened again and Rusty Zidek came in. He pulled off his worn, brown, cowboy hat, smoothed down his gray hair and brushed his impressive cookie duster of a mustache. In spite of being ninety-six years old, Rusty managed to keep his finger on the pulse of what happened in Jasper Gulch. He and his Mule were often seen putt-putting down Main Street as Rusty sought out people to talk to and things to find out. Hannah wondered what he wanted from her today.

Rusty settled himself slowly into a chair beside Robin. She turned to him, asking him questions about Jasper Gulch. From the way Robin scribbled notes as he talked, Hannah assumed they would be busy awhile.

The phone rang just then and with an apologetic look toward Brody, Hannah answered it and set the application form for the booth on top of the counter, next to Brody's hand.

As she did, she noticed Lilibeth had captured his attention again by batting long, thick eyelashes that Hannah suspected were glued on rather than natural. Lilibeth had her head cocked to one side, her finger resting on her cheek, her eyelashes fluttering, her smile showing off perfectly spaced teeth.

And for a moment, Hannah was surprised herself that Lilibeth hadn't won the Miss Jasper Gulch contest. But what surprised Hannah even more was the faint uptick of jealousy Lilibeth's flirtation created in her.

"So I hope I filled this out right," Brody said, looking back at Hannah when she was done with her phone call. As he handed her the paper, their fingers brushed. A spark of awareness tingled down her arm and then his eyes locked with hers. His smile seemed to soften and deepen and her heart did a goofy little dance in her chest.

Then reality hit. She couldn't help comparing herself, a harried mother of two toddlers who barely had time to run a brush through her hair, let alone apply makeup, to fresh-faced Lilibeth, who looked put together enough to be in a fashion magazine. Though she doubted Brody would be attracted to a nineteen-year-old, the comparison still made her feel old and worn-out.

"Looks good, Mr. Harcourt," Hannah said, pushing down the futile emotions. "I look forward to seeing what the firefighters come up with."

"And if I have any questions?"

"Just come to me." Hannah hoped she sounded businesslike and not like a breathless schoolgirl in the presence of her crush. "Have a good day." Then she looked past him as Robin got up to walk toward the counter.

"Can I help you, Robin?" Hannah asked, effectively dismissing both Brody and Lilibeth.

Brody paused a moment as if he did, indeed, have a question. But then Robin stepped up to the counter and he turned and stepped aside, smiling at a joke Lilibeth was telling him.

"Nice-looking couple," Robin said as she set her folder of papers on the divider.

They're not a couple, Hannah wanted to say, but she stopped herself. What did it matter to her that Robin thought Brody and Lilibeth were together?

"I returned those papers you lent me," Robin continued, handing an envelope back to Hannah. "Though the documents were interesting, I was hoping to find out more about some of the occupations of the extended Shaw family. Olivia said to talk to you."

Hannah bit her lip, thinking. "I'll see what I can find. Mayor Shaw might have that information, as well."

"I don't want to bother him," Robin murmured.

"Don't worry. I'll take care of it," Hannah assured her, then had to apologize as she answered the phone again. Her day didn't look as if it would be slowing down anytime soon.

Or her life. She gave another quick glance at Brody,

holding open the door for Lilibeth, then turned her attention back to her work. She had no space in her life for a man like him.

Well, that didn't go as well as he had hoped.

Brody Harcourt dropped his hat on his head and heaved out a sigh as he held the door of the town hall open for Lilibeth Shoemaker. He had been the one to pitch the idea of setting up a booth for the firefighters at the fair precisely because he had hoped he could spend some time with Hannah Douglas.

Brody had been a senior in high school when he and his parents first moved to their new ranch in Jasper Gulch, and already then Hannah Douglas, with her gentle smile and perky demeanor, had caught his attention. But other than one summer when he was graduated and she and David had briefly split up, she had always been David Douglas's girl.

Now she was David Douglas's widow and the mother of his twins and, from the way she had just treated him, still not interested in him.

"If I make a basket, you'll have to make sure to bid on it," Lilibeth was saying to him. "I'll let you know what it looks like."

"Isn't that against the rules?" he said as he tugged his cell phone out of his pocket.

Lilibeth simpered at him, then shrugged. "My sisters do it all the time."

"I might be too busy to bid anyway," Brody said, giving a quick glance at the screen. A text from his friend Dylan. He was already at the café and waiting for him.

"Well, you set some time aside for me," Lilibeth gave him a coy smile, then sashayed down Main Street.

"She's quite the spitfire, isn't she?"

Rusty Zidek's gravelly voice behind Brody made him spin around. "Yeah, she is," he agreed, looking back at Lilibeth, who shot him one last look over her shoulder as she stepped into her car.

"She seems overly upset lately about not winning the Miss Jasper Gulch contest," Rusty continued, stroking his mustache, his grin showing the glint of a gold tooth.

"Her pride probably got bruised. Two of her sisters won before and I think she's feeling the sting of sisterly competition." Brody gave the elderly man a quick smile. "I have two sisters. They're always one-upping each other. Clothes, boyfriends, jobs."

"So was she nattering to Hannah about the contest, then?" Rusty asked, his voice nonchalant. But Brody caught a flicker of intensity in his eyes and was curious about his furtive movements.

"All I know is that she wanted to find out more about the Miss Jasper Gulch contest. Claimed it was rigged. She was asking if Hannah could access the minutes from the council meetings." Brody felt like a tattletale, but he was curious where Rusty was going with this.

Rusty nodded slowly, as if digesting this information. "Well, we'll need to discuss that later." Then he looked up at Brody, his expression serious. "And I heard that you've said you would be willing to be part of the Time Capsule Committee."

"Yeah, about that…" Brody paused a moment, thinking of the work ahead of him and his father on the ranch. They had just expanded and were busier than previous years. "Not so sure I can do it."

"We could use your help trying to find the town's missing time capsule. Deputy Calloway had his concerns about your being on the committee, but he did say if you were willing, he would overlook them."

Brody knew exactly what those concerns were. He and Deputy Calloway had had a few run-ins during Brody's wilder years. But Rusty's comment made him uncertain, his pride battling with his ongoing desire to prove himself trustworthy.

"Hannah is the new secretary," Rusty added with a little nudge of his elbow.

Brody held Rusty's gaze, his piercing blue eyes nestled in a valley of wrinkles, a road map of his years and experience. Rusty had seen a lot coming and going in this town, and Brody knew the older man didn't miss much.

"Well, that has a certain appeal," he admitted. No sense being less than straight up with someone like Rusty.

"Kind of thought it might," Rusty said with a smug look. "We started meeting in the late afternoon, to accommodate Hannah's schedule. Our next meeting is Wednesday."

"I'll be there. Now, if you'll excuse me, I have to meet Dylan at Great Gulch Grub."

"See you later," Rusty said, then turned and walked across the street to the bakery where Brody saw his camouflage-colored Mule was parked.

Brody followed him but ducked into Great Gulch Grub. He saw Dylan sitting at a table toward the back of the noisy café, his hands clasped on either side of his shaved head, glowering at a large manual lying on the scarred, Formica-covered table.

"Can I please get a coffee and a piece of Vincente's amazing apple pie?" Brody asked Mert, who stood behind the counter. Behind her he could hear Vincente singing snatches of an unfamiliar song. Probably some opera thing that he seemed to enjoy.

Mert's hair was pulled back in her perpetual bun, but this late in the day a few hanks of hair had come loose and hung around her narrow face.

"What am I, your wife?" she quipped, giving the empty counter a wipe with the cloth she held.

"I still live in hope," Brody said, sweeping his hat off his head and placing it on his chest.

"You should get your own in time for the Old Tyme wedding going on next month," Mert teased. "I thought a romantic like you would be all over that event."

Brody just laughed, Mert's innocent comment making him think of Hannah. "Not yet, Mert. Not yet."

"Don't worry, cowboy, I know your future bride is out there. And if she's not ready, we'll find someone for you."

"*That* makes me worry," he said, pointing a finger at her. "I can find my own wife, thank you very much." Then, before Mert could carry the conversation any further, he strode to the back of the café, greeting a few of the people he knew and dropping into an empty chair across from his friend.

"Troubles with the motorbike?" he asked, glancing over the pages Dylan was studying.

"Yeah. Something with the manifold." Dylan sighed. "Sure wish you hadn't sold yours. I could've scammed some parts from it."

"Everything has its season and the motorbike's was over."

"We sure had some good times with them," Dylan said.

Brody's thoughts ticked back to those trips with Dylan, roaring through the countryside, carefree and foolish. He also remembered how happy his parents were when he sold the bike.

"So, thoughts about the booth for the fair?" he asked, changing the subject. "I already picked one out."

"Me and the other guys were thinking we should get a corner one so we can park the fire truck behind it. Kids can sit in it. They love that kind of thing."

"Here you go, cowboy," Mert said to Brody, setting his pie and coffee in front of him. "Enjoy, and let me know when you're ready to go wife shopping."

"I'm fine," Brody said with a grin. He picked up the fork and dug into his pie, his mouth watering. "I'll have to go back and talk to Hannah again and change the booth if you want a corner one," he said to Dylan between mouthfuls of cinnamon-laced apple pie.

The idea appealed, but he wanted to take a day to regroup and find another way to turn on the charm.

"You could talk to her now," Dylan said, raising his chin toward the door.

Hannah came in, glanced around the café, then seemed to hesitate when she saw him, the smile on her face fading away. Brody knew the only empty table in the café was beside him and Dylan.

Her hesitation stung. A little. Though he knew she was a widow, he had nurtured a faint hope that maybe, eventually, he could let her see there were other fish in the sea. Him being one of the fish.

Then, with a gentle smile for Dylan and a polite one for him, she sat down at the empty table, her back to Brody.

Dylan raised his eyebrow, as if in question, and nodded toward Hannah again. "Here's our chance." He leaned over to look past Brody. "Hey, Mrs. Douglas. Brody needs to talk to you." Then Dylan nudged Brody under the table with his foot and Brody had no choice but to deal with this.

With a glare at his friend, Brody wiped the piecrust crumbs off his face, put on a smile and turned around in his chair.

"Hi again," he said, leaning his arm across the back of the wooden chair. "So. About that booth. Could we make a change?"

Hannah held his gaze and then looked down at the cell phone she clutched as if she needed to do something with it. "Depends on what you want to do."

Still not too eager to talk to him, he noted. He pulled in a breath and pushed on. "Dylan and I were just talking. Could we snag a corner booth instead? We were hoping to set up a fire truck behind it if there's room."

That caught her attention. Her subsequent smile and excitement reignited a glimmer of hope. "That would be a great idea," she said.

"We thought the kids would like that, too," Brody said, encouraged by her enthusiasm. "We could get some little fire hats to give away."

"What do you think of getting someone to take pictures of the kids with their hats on standing by the truck?" Her infectious smile increased her appeal. Her dark eyes lit up, and the light from the window behind her made her brown hair shine. She wore it loose and it flowed over her shoulders. Like melted chocolate.

"I think Scottie Sawchuk at the station has a good camera. We could get him set up. What do you think of selling people the pictures?"

"As part of the fund-raiser. Great idea." Her eyes sparkled with eagerness and a full, genuine smile curved her soft lips.

And dived into his heart and settled there.

"Perfect. If you could get us that corner stall, we're in business."

"I'll do whatever I can," she said.

Brody nodded, unable to ignore the knock of awareness he felt. She blinked, and her smile slowly faded. A cloud slid across the sun and the light left with her smile, followed by an awkward silence. Brody felt his brain seize up as he tried to find something clever to say.

"If there's nothing more..." Hannah let the sentence hang, giving him the perfect opportunity to capitalize on the moment, but nope. Still nothing.

Since when was he tongue-tied in the presence of a woman?

Since it was Hannah Douglas. And though his mind was blank, he couldn't keep his eyes off her.

"No. I think that's it," he said finally.

"Then I'll let you get back to your dessert," she said.

Her words were polite and her voice cool and once again Brody got the impression she was trying to get rid of him. Then she turned away and Brody returned to his pie.

"So I guess we've got that settled then," Dylan said, closing his book and looking up at his friend, thankfully unaware of Brody making unsuccessful googly eyes at Hannah Douglas. "You stopping at the hall before you go to the ranch?"

"I need to pick up a shirt I left behind there after our last call to Alfie Hart's place."

"Still can't believe you were about to go into that barn for his dog."

Brody just shrugged as he took another bite of pie. The fire Dylan talked about had been straightforward until Alfie called out that his dog was inside the barn. Alfie was a bachelor and he and his dog were inseparable. Alfie had run to the barn with the idea of getting the dog out himself. Brody had pulled him back and had promised he would check it out. But as he put on his mask and headed into the building, the dog came charging around the other side.

"Someday you'll have a reason not to be such a daredevil," Dylan said, closing the manual and leaning back in his booth. "Like a girlfriend." He gave Brody a smirk as if he knew that Brody was far too aware of Hannah sitting right behind him.

Brody just ignored him, wolfed down the last of his pie, chased it with coffee and stood.

"Let's go." Brody pulled out his wallet, fished a few bills out and dropped them on the table.

But before he left, he chanced another look at Hannah. And was surprised to see her looking at him, her eyes holding a question.

Then she turned away, effectively dismissing him. Again.

"She's pretty, isn't she?" Dylan asked Brody as they walked down Main Street back to the fire station.

"Who?"

Dylan nudged him with his elbow. "You know exactly who I'm talking about. Hannah Douglas. I know you've always liked her."

Brody shrugged off his friend's comment, preferring not to go back to that time. "That was many years and a lot of experiences ago."

"Just as well. Those twins are a big responsibility. You want to date that woman, you've got huge shoes to fill."

"David had big feet?" Brody asked, deliberately misunderstanding what Dylan was saying.

Dylan seemed to ignore his remark. "David Douglas

was a good guy," he said, his voice quiet. Almost reverent. "A man that good shouldn't have died on some Afghani field by a roadside. Lousy bombers making Hannah a widow and single mother."

"Only the good die young," Brody murmured.

"He was always the first to volunteer for stuff. Always helping people." Dylan was quiet a moment, as if remembering all the good things David Douglas had done. "Remember that summer when I was thinking of quitting my job as a carpenter? Leaving Jasper Gulch?"

"Was that the summer we cruised down the Oregon coast on our motorbikes?" Brody sighed. "I don't think we drove under ninety that whole trip."

"Yup. That summer. I never told you what happened when I came back from that trip because I felt embarrassed."

"About what?"

Dylan shrugged, then crossed over the street. "You and I were pretty wild then. Neither of us attended church anymore."

Though his relationship with God was an integral part of Brody's life now, for many years the faith he had been born and raised with had been relegated to the "someday" corner of his life. The same place the wife and the three kids were always put. Somehow, in his wilder years, he had always assumed when he was ready for God, the rest would fall into place, as well.

Now he was twenty-nine and still no closer to finding a wife than he had been then.

"Well, I was feeling down," Dylan was saying.

Brody punched him in the shoulder. "That was why we went on the trip. To get you out of that funk."

"Trouble was, it didn't help. I didn't know what

I wanted. David came over when we got back from our trip. He said he was concerned about me. Said he wanted to pray with me. It felt a little funny, especially after all the goofing around you and I had done, but I said yes." Dylan shrugged, as if still self-conscious about what had happened. "Anyhow, praying with him gave me such peace and comfort. He came once a week just to talk and see how things were with me. He encouraged me to start coming back to church."

Brody felt a flash of guilt at the memory. What a contrast. One friend who figured going crazy was the way to fix the problems in Dylan's life. The other, who wasn't even as close to Dylan as Brody was, knowing the right thing to do.

"So that's why you started going back to church," Brody said quietly as he punched in the pass code to get into the fire station. "I always wondered."

"It was. We talked about work and jobs and he told me being a carpenter was a good thing to do. That building houses was important. That maybe I should find a way to give to the community, as well. Step outside of myself. And that's when I volunteered for this gig," he finished, his wave taking in the fire hall as they walked up the stairs to the dorms where they slept and kept their personal gear.

Brody felt a moment of letdown. "I always thought you signed up because of me."

"Kind of, but mostly because of David. He did a lot of good for a lot of people."

And Hannah, as well.

The hardest fire to fight is an old flame, Brody thought, reality falling into his life like the thud of an ax. He always had a vague feeling Hannah was out of reach.

Now he knew for sure.

* * *

By the time Hannah locked the doors of town hall, the pain behind her eyes had blossomed into a full-blown headache. Her feet ached and her back was sore and she generally just felt sorry for herself after such a busy day. But as she trudged across Main Street to her apartment, she stopped her moments of self-pity.

Forgive me, Lord, she prayed. *Help me be thankful for what I have.*

The twins were healthy and she had the support of her friends and family.

But I'm alone.

The taunting thought worried at her moment of peace. Truth to tell, her loneliness had taken on a new hue the past few months. Losing David so soon after they married had been difficult. He had been a part of her life since she was in grade school. They had dated since the ninth grade. He was all she had ever known.

When he had signed up for the army, she had tried to be supportive. But when he proposed marriage just before he had received his orders to ship out, she had struggled with his urgency to get married. Her parents had simply told her to go with her heart. If she had followed their advice, she would have put off the marriage. She would have waited, but when David's parents had added their voices to his, they created a pressure she was unable to withstand.

Two months later, she was a widow and pregnant with twins, unable to indulge in second thoughts. Her life had been a whirlwind of uncertain emotions and busyness ever since.

And in the past few months, a sense of loneliness had been added to the emotional stew.

Her thoughts slipped back to Brody as she opened

the door leading to the stairs up to her apartment. Was it her overactive imagination, or maybe her lonely heart, that thought he had been flirting with her?

No sooner did that thought form than she heard Chrissy's wails growing louder as she walked up the narrow stairs. Hannah took the last flight two at a time, digging in her purse for the key to the door.

Inside her apartment her mother sat in a wooden rocking chair holding a sobbing Chrissy, Corey clinging to her denim skirt, also crying. Chrissy's blond curls clung to her forehead, and as Hannah closed the door, the little girl leaned away from her grandmother and reached out for Hannah, tears flowing down her scrunched-up cheeks.

"Oh, honey," Hannah said, taking the hot bundle of sadness from her mother and tucking Chrissy's warm head under her chin. "You're still not feeling good, are you?" Chrissy released a few more sobs then quieted. Hannah dropped to the floor, shifted Chrissy to one arm, then scooped Corey up with her other arm. As he snuggled into her, blessed silence descended in the apartment.

"How was your day?" her mother asked, still sitting in the chair, her head resting against the back. Her glasses were smudged and her hair mussed and Hannah suspected the orange stain down the front of her shirt was from lunch.

"You look tired, Mom," she said, guilt falling like a familiar weight on her shoulders. "I should have come here at lunchtime instead of going to the café."

Her mother waved off her objections and smiled. "You needed the break. Your father came and helped me with the children. We had fun, though I'm sorry I didn't have time to clean up."

Hannah took in the toys scattered around the apartment with its mismatched furniture given to her by friends and people from the community. When she imagined becoming a mother and bringing grandchildren into her parents' lives, this was not the picture she had envisioned.

"And how was your day?" her mother repeated.

"It was busy," Hannah replied, nuzzling Chrissy, who lay quietly in her arms now, her chubby hands clutching at Hannah's sweater. "We received far more people signing up for the fair than originally estimated."

"That will be good. I just hope the committee doesn't listen to all those people who want to fix the bridge," her mother said as she folded her arms over her chest. "I much prefer to see the museum we had talked about for so long finally getting built. We don't need that bridge," her mother continued. "Some things are better left alone."

Hannah pressed a kiss to Corey's damp head, making a noncommittal sound. The entire bridge versus museum controversy and where the fund-raising money should go was starting to split the community. As an employee of the town, Hannah had found it best to simply listen and not get drawn into either side of the discussion.

"Did you get to the park today?" Hannah asked, diverting her mother's attention elsewhere. The sun, shining through the windows of town hall had taunted her all day and, once again, made her wish she didn't have to work. Made her wish she could live off the small pension she received from the military. Because David had barely graduated training and because he had signed up for the minimum of life insurance, Hannah was managing by the thinnest of margins. David's insurance payout was in a savings account she slowly added to each month.

In a year or so she might have enough saved up to buy her and her children a little house. Their own place. The twins would have a yard and be able to play outside. Though her parents had offered for her to move in with them, she valued her independence too much. In the meantime, she made do with this apartment and working as much as she dared.

"No. Chrissy was tired," her mother said. "And I just wanted to stay in the apartment."

"I'm sorry, Mother," Hannah said. "I wasn't trying to make you feel bad."

"I know, honey." Her mother sighed as she stood. "I wished I could have gone out with them, but there it is." She glanced over at the tiny kitchen beside them. "And I didn't do the dishes from lunch, either. By the time I got the children down for their nap, I needed one myself."

Hannah waved off her concern, fighting her own weariness and another surge of guilt. "I don't expect you to do everything," Hannah said. "I'm just thankful you and Dad help out as much as you do."

"We're glad we can do this for you." Leaning over, she brushed a gentle kiss over Hannah's cheek. "You've been such a brave girl, dealing with losing David. Never a word of complaint." Her mother kissed each of the twins in turn and then straightened. "You know we pray for you every day when your father and I have our devotional time."

"I know." This created another flush of shame. The only prayers Hannah seemed to have time for were the panicky ones that were either *please, please, please* or *thank you, thank you, thank you.* Her faith life, of late, had become fallow and parched. "And someday

I'll make it back to church." She wouldn't soon forget the last time she had made the attempt with her toddlers in tow. It had been a disaster.

"I know you will." Her mother gave her a smile, then walked over to the closet by the front door to collect her coat. "I'd better get going. I'll be back tomorrow," she said, and then, with another wave, her mother left.

The apartment felt suddenly empty. Hannah fought down the usual twinge of loneliness and clutched her babies tighter. She had her kids. She had her family.

That should be enough.

She set the twins down on the floor to play, but as she stood to clean the kitchen, she stopped by the window overlooking Main Street and the fire station across the street from the hardware store.

Images of Brody Harcourt slipped through her mind. She shook them off. Brody was better matched with a young, pretty girl who had no attachments. No history.

And she was better off with someone more solid and settled.

If she could ever find anyone like that who would also be willing to take on another man's children.

Such a silly dream, she thought, turning away from the window and back to her reality.

Chapter Two

Brody parked his truck in front of his cabin, turned off his engine and dragged his hands over his face as if smoothing out his thoughts.

All the way back to the ranch he had been thinking about what Dylan had said about David. When he heard Hannah was planning the fair, he was the one who had pitched the idea to his buddies at the fire station to set up a booth. All so he could find a reason to go talk to her.

When Rusty told him that Hannah was the secretary of the Time Capsule Committee, he thought this was another opportunity.

Then Dylan had told him what he had about David and once again Brody felt he was wasting his time.

He looked over at his parents' house perched up on the hill. His father had built it for his mother after they had talked about expanding the ranch. Brody had been dating a girl he met in Bozeman and he thought things were getting serious between them and he and his father started making plans for the future. Trista was perfect in every way. Young. Pretty. Loved the ranch. Loved horses. Loved him. Or so he'd thought until her old boyfriend came back into town and she started pulling away. Brody had no desire to play second fiddle to anyone, so they both decided it was best if they broke up.

His mother had been more brokenhearted than he had been. Which made him wonder just how much he had cared for Trista.

He had dated a couple of girls since then but nothing seemed to take. Somehow, in some twisted part of his mind, he compared every woman he ever met to Hannah.

Then David died.

Brody had bided his time, giving her space, and thought maybe now was the time. He had figured wrong.

Brody got out of the truck, a chilly breeze fingering down his neck. Fall was coming and with it the work of gathering the cattle.

He stepped inside his cabin and dropped the mail he had picked up on a table just inside the door. He was about to leave again but took a moment, looking around the interior, trying to see it through others' eyes.

Hannah's eyes?

It was the main ranch house when his parents moved here, but the family had only lived here until a new, larger home was built. When Brody graduated high school, he'd moved back here, preferring to have his own place. Though he had spent a number of years away from Jasper Gulch, traveling, he always knew he would come back to the ranch to stay. For the past six years this cabin had been his home.

An old leather couch, chair and love seat, all cast off from his parents, crowded around a woodstove in the living room. Opposite them stood a table with four mismatched chairs parked under a large window overlooking the ranch. The kitchen area was to his right. It had a few cabinets and a fridge and stove, also taken from his parents' home when they upgraded and renovated the main ranch house. Between the dining and living area was a hallway leading to two small rooms and a bathroom/laundry room.

For a moment he wondered what Hannah would think of this house.

He caught himself and stopped that thought before it had a chance to take root. He had to be practical, and Dylan's comments about taking on the twins and the ensuing responsibility were a reminder of what came with Hannah. The history he would have to compete with. Besides, Hannah didn't seem very interested.

He left to see where his father was. He strode up the graveled walk to his parents' house, a two-and-a-half-story home built into a hillside and surrounded by pine trees.

He knocked on the large double doors, then, without waiting for an answer, walked inside. The open foyer was piled with old boots, clothes and boxes of various sizes. All evidence of an ongoing cleaning operation his mother had undertaken in the past few months but was having a hard time finishing. He toed off his boots and dropped his hat on top of a pile of boxes labeled Jennifer and Sophia. His sisters who were both living in Denver.

His mother sat at the eating counter of the kitchen to the right of the entrance, hunched over her iPad, her elbow resting on the granite countertop, supporting her chin.

"Where's Dad?" he asked, looking past her to the open living room that took up most of the house. His father's leather recliner, sitting on one side of the rock-covered fireplace, only held a stack of papers. His mother's, on the other side, held her latest project, a scarf she had been knitting under Julie Shaw's tutelage.

"He headed out to check the high pasture," she said, flicking through a series of pictures. "He took the old ranch truck."

"He'd better not be moving cows," Brody said, frowning. His father had recently had a bout of heart issues and though he claimed he was feeling better, Brody didn't want him doing the hard work he used to.

"Dad said he would wait until Lewis was back, which won't be until after next weekend." His mother swiped her finger over the screen of the iPad again, smiling at what she was seeing.

Lewis was their hired hand. He had gone to Helena for the weekend courting a woman he had met at the rodeo held in Jasper Gulch a couple of months ago.

"What are you looking at?" Brody asked, pulling a tall stool up beside her.

His mother sighed lightly and turned the iPad toward him. "Aunt Kirsty sent me some pictures of her newest grandson, Owen." This was said with a sigh tinged with envy. "The newest of six." She looked up at him and emitted a second sigh meant to create a hint, but Brody simply patted her on the shoulder and grinned.

"Sophia sounds like she and her guy are getting serious," he said, hoping to shift his mother's attention from him to his sister. "Someday they might give you grandkids."

She looked back at the picture of the chubby baby boy sucking on his fingers wearing a blue-and-white-striped shirt. "So, how was your morning? Did you get your stuff all set up for the fair?" Hopefully the shift in topic meant that was the end of that train of thought.

His mother had been getting all nesty lately, dropping hints left and right.

"Yeah. Looks like it will be a big deal. Lots of exhibitors."

"This centennial sure has made a lot of people busy. The rodeo, the baseball game, the fair." She sighed and her smile grew wistful. "The Old Tyme wedding next month."

She angled her head and Brody knew his mother's mental train had merely taken a short side trip and was back on track.

"Maybe you could participate." Her tone was teasing, but Brody sensed the hope behind it.

For some reason, his mind immediately went to Hannah, imagining her as a bride.

Really? He shook the thought aside.

"Yeah. Like I'm going to find someone by that time," he returned with a grin.

"Your father and I met and were married in two weeks," his mother said. "You've got time. Mayor Shaw has a couple of real nice daughters. Pretty, too."

"Julie is engaged," he said.

And he was sure Mayor Shaw, a man very protective of his daughters, would not allow Book-it Brody to have anything to do with Faith, his last single daughter. Besides, while Faith was pretty and fun, she didn't hold any attraction for him.

An image of Hannah slipped into his mind. How she bantered with him. How her eyes had lit up when they'd had that conversation in the café.

"What are you smiling about?" his mother asked.

Brody gave his mother a wry glance. Trust her to catch the tiniest shifts in his mood.

"Nothing," he lied.

"Well, you better start thinking about my need for grandkids. I want to have them before I'm too old to enjoy them."

Brody laughed and patted his mother on the shoulder. "Just give me time," he said. "Things will work in God's own good time."

His mother sighed. "I know. I just wish God would let me know when that time will be. So I can start a new knitting project. Julie Shaw just put some new wool up on her website that would be perfect for a baby sweater."

"Whoa. Stop there," Brody said. "One step at a time."

"I know. I'm just nudging you a little toward that first step," she said, turning back to her iPad.

Brody looked over at the pictures and smiled at the toothless grin of the little boy. Of their own accord, his thoughts shifted to Hannah and her twins.

And on the heels of that came Dylan's comment about taking on that responsibility. He wasn't so sure he was ready for that.

"I'd like to call this meeting to order," Deputy Cal Calloway announced, glancing over the gathering. Rusty Zidek sat across the table from Hannah, fingering his long, gray mustache as he looked over the agenda in front of him. Abigail Rose sat beside him, frowning at Hannah. "And I would like to thank Mrs. Douglas for agreeing to take over from Miss Rose to be our new secretary. Abigail asked to step down, stating her obligation to the Centennial Committee, but we're glad she decided to stay with us."

This netted Hannah a wink from Rusty and a sigh of relief from Cord Shaw. Cal gave her a quick smile of thanks, his blue eyes twinkling at her, then he returned to the agenda.

The meeting was being held in one of the smaller rooms adjacent to the council chambers. As Hannah opened the laptop she used to take minutes for the town meetings, she glanced at the time on the top of the screen.

Hannah had promised her mother she would be home by five. It was three-thirty now and she needed to stop at the pharmacy to pick up medication for Chrissy, whose teething pain still hadn't settled. Plus, she needed more laundry detergent. And juice and a new mop. Her old one had broken on her as she rushed around the apartment last night cleaning up while the twins were sleeping.

As her mental list expanded, Hannah felt another resurgence of sorrow mingled with anger at David's death. If they hadn't gotten married so quickly she wouldn't have gotten pregnant and she wouldn't be rushing around right now juggling all these obligations on her own.

Hannah dismissed that thought as quickly as it was formulated. She loved her babies. Fiercely. It was just that she wished her babies had a father and that they could have known David.

Her thoughts were broken off by the door opening. As it had the last time, she saw Brody Harcourt, and her heart gave a little jump. It had been almost a week since he had come into the town hall and somehow, ever since then, he had been on her mind. The fire station was only a couple of buildings away and she had caught the occasional glimpse of him when she returned to her place for lunch. But he hadn't come back to the town hall since that day.

Then, to her dismay, he pulled out the empty chair beside her and sat down. She gave him a nod of acknowledgment, then dragged her attention back to the flickering cursor on the blank screen. She typed a header for the document. Deleted it and started again when she realized her fingers were on the wrong keys. Seriously, she had to get her head in the game. It wasn't as if Brody was new in town and they had just met.

No, but it was the first time since David's death any man had shown interest in her.

And you shut him down.

And so she should have. She was a widow with two children who required all her time and attention. And Brody Harcourt was the kind of man who liked to take risks. Not the kind of person she should be attracted to.

She swallowed and focused on Deputy Cal Calloway, who was making a few additions to the agenda. Hannah started typing, mentally sorting and filtering what needed to go in the minutes from what was being said.

"The first item we need to deal with is if we need to do anything more with this note we received."

"Which note is this?" Brody asked.

"I'll bring you up to speed, Brody," Cal said, spreading a piece of paper in front of him. "Cord received this letter a while back. We're not sure what to do about it." He rested a hand on the table as he looked down at the paper. "It says, 'If you want to know what happened to your time capsule, you need to think about L.S.' Now, we aren't sure who L.S. is, but we have a suspicion it might be Lilibeth Shoemaker."

"How did you get the note?" Brody asked.

"It came anonymously to Abigail," Cord spoke up. "Sent in a dirty envelope. No return address. No idea who brought it."

"Me and the mayor asked Olivia to look into what was in that time capsule," Abigail put in, looking self-important. "And we both thought we should keep an eye on Lilibeth."

"So now we need to decide what to do about this," Cal said. "As you know, the sheriff's office is stretched thin, so we're hoping this committee could help us with this."

"I say we confront her," Abigail said, inspecting her electric-blue nails, her glasses glinting in the bright lights of the meeting room. "She was pretty angry about losing that beauty contest. I'm sure she did it to get even and she needs to know you can't steal stuff belonging to the town."

"Now, Abigail, we don't know for sure she is a suspect in spite of her being upset," Cal admonished her. "And whoever sent this note wasn't ready or willing to show his or her face. It could just be someone who has an ax to grind with Lilibeth."

"Or it could be someone who knows something," Abigail pressed.

Rusty leaned forward, looking over at Brody. "Say, Mr. Harcourt, I noticed at the town hall the other day that Ms. Shoemaker seemed mighty interested in you."

Hannah was surprised at the twinge of jealousy Rusty's comment gave her. And why she should even feel that way.

She thought of their conversation in the café last week. How, for a moment, she had felt it again. That slow curl of attraction she hadn't felt in years.

Brody created a completely different set of emotions that made her feel as if she was being unfaithful to David's memory.

"She's a flirt, that's all," Brody said, his voice disinterested.

"She's never flirted with me," Cord said, grinning as he leaned forward to look past Hannah at Brody.

"Maybe it's because I'm a romantic, whereas you're a hardened bachelor who doesn't believe in love," Brody retorted. "Which makes me wonder why you're on that Old Tyme Wedding Committee."

"It's *because* I'm a hardened bachelor," Cord said with a laugh. "I can view things objectively." Cord looked back down at the note in front of him, then over to Brody again. "As for Lilibeth, I think you should capitalize on her interest in you. Maybe see if you can find out what she knows. Turn on that Harcourt charm."

"I think that's a great idea," Abigail said, suddenly coming to life. "You could cozy up to her. Find out what she's been up to. You're a good-looking guy, she'd be interested in you."

"I dunno about the good-looking part," Cord drawled. He gave Hannah a little nudge with his elbow. "We need a second opinion. What do you think, Hannah? Would you be interested in a guy like Brody?"

Hannah could only stare at Cord, her mind going blank as she struggled to think what to say.

"I'm—I'm not Lilibeth Shoemaker, so—so I can't— can't say." She clamped her lips on her stammering response and turned her attention back to the laptop in front of her, wishing her cheeks didn't feel so warm. She was sure she was blushing.

"I think we should follow through on the note," Rusty said, folding his gnarled hands over each other, his eyes narrowing as his piercing gaze moved to each member of the committee. "See where it takes us."

"I'm not going to flirt with Lilibeth," Brody said, a note of finality in his voice. "It's not fair to her because I'm not even interested in her."

His adamant tone created a surprising serenity in Hannah and his "not interested" comment, a tremble of hope.

"And we all know that Book-it Brody doesn't look back or go where he's not wanted," Cord said with a hint of a smile. "Too proud."

"But Lilibeth is the only one in town we know of with the initials L.S.," Abigail continued, obviously not willing to let this go. "And what was she doing at town hall?"

Hannah assumed the question was addressed to her. "She was asking about the Miss Jasper Gulch contest," she said. "She claimed it was rigged and wanted to find out more about it."

"See. There you go. She's snooping around. She's hiding something." Abigail slapped her hand on the table as she turned to Brody. "I think you'd better check her out, Brody."

"I have a better idea," Cord said, his drawl deepening. "Why don't we get Mr. Harcourt and Mrs. Douglas to speak with her together. That way she won't be suspicious and it would satisfy Brody's tender sensibilities."

Brody shook his head, wondering what Cord was up to. "I don't know about that, either—"

"I think that's a great idea." Rusty cut into Brody's protest, granting Hannah and Brody an avuncular look. "Why don't you two take her out for coffee in the next couple of days. Feel her out about the time capsule. It'd be better if the two of you do it. Like Cord said, she won't be as suspicious."

"I agree," said Deputy Calloway before Hannah could lodge her own protest. "We need to deal with this note, and this is the most discreet way to find out if Lilibeth has anything to do with the disappearance of the time capsule. Now, let's move on to the next item on the agenda."

Hannah's fingers automatically typed the words as the meeting went on, but the entire time she typed she was aware of Brody sitting beside her and the "date" they were supposed to arrange.

Looked as if she didn't have much choice. Spending time with Brody was probably not the best idea. She would simply have to remember that in spite of her feelings for Brody, she was a mother first and foremost.

Her thoughts flipped back to the conversation she had overheard between Dylan and Brody.

Brody's job had so many risks. She didn't think he was the kind of man she should allow her heart to follow.

Chapter Three

"Here's my donation for the basket auction." Annette Lakey set a large, cellophane-covered basket on the divider. Bright purple ribbons tied off the top of a basket loaded with bottles of shampoo, lotion, conditioner, a nail kit and assorted other goodies that Hannah assumed came from Annette's hair salon, the Cutting Edge. Though Annette was a walking advertisement for her own salon with her black-and-pink-streaked hair, she also knew her clientele well enough and was a whiz with perms and basic cuts. "I also stuck in a gift certificate for a haircut."

"This is excellent," Hannah said, getting up to take the basket. "I'll put it with the others." She would have to bring some more of the baskets to Abigail's today. She'd been storing the premade theme baskets in her apartment.

"Do you think you'll get your fifty baskets? That still seems like a lot."

By asking for fifty picnic baskets for the auction, the Jasper Gulch Centennial Committee wanted to tie in with the World's Largest Old Tyme Wedding scheduled for next month, where fifty couples would be exchanging vows.

"We're getting there. But a lot of people seem to want to make themed baskets, which helps."

"Are you making one? For that special someone?" Annette asked with a gleam in her dark eyes.

Hannah's thoughts slipped to Brody Harcourt, but she shook her head, flashing Annette a tight smile. "I'm making one, but just for the fund-raiser. Not anyone special."

"Of course. I forgot about David," Annette said, sympathy lacing her voice. "I'm so sorry." More people in town seemed to treat her with a type of deference. As if losing David exalted her to a position above any other widow in the town.

Trouble was, Hannah had forgotten about David, too.

"Anyhow, I hope the committee doesn't get pulled into channeling the money from this fund-raiser to the museum." Annette said. "I mean, we've had two big events already that brought people to town and more coming. Tony and I were talking about it last night. We both agree the bridge should be fixed. It would mean more opportunities for his vet business, as well. I wish people would stop living in the past and move on." Annette shrugged, then slung her bright pink, oversize bag over her shoulder. "It's time the people of Jasper Gulch realize we need more than one road in and out of this burg."

"You aren't the first to make that comment."

"I know there are people who are spooked by the fact that Lucy's car ran off the bridge and she died all those years ago. But that happened so long ago that it's time for the town to move on," Annette added with a toss of her streaked hair. "Anyway, I better get going.

Tony and I are going out for dinner tonight. You make sure to pass the message on to Mayor Shaw, will you?"

"I'll let him know," Hannah assured her.

"And next time you have a couple of hours, come into the salon. I'll fix you up real pretty," Annette said.

Hannah self-consciously lifted her hand to tuck her hair behind her ear. She knew she was overdue for a cut. The last time she had sat in a beauty salon had been the day of her wedding. And that was a hasty appointment almost two years ago. For the most part, she wore her hair long and pulled back, and trimmed it herself in the mirror. Much easier with her busy life. "Thanks, but—"

"Some highlights and a bit of shaping would be perfect for you. You'd be adorable with bangs." Annette pulled a card out of her capacious bag and set it on the counter. "I'll even do it free. Anything for the wife of one of our brave soldiers."

Her sympathetic smile made Hannah even more self-conscious.

She just returned Annette's smile as the young woman tossed off a quick wave, then walked away. She reached for the heavy wooden door leading outside just as it swung open, sending in a shaft of afternoon sunlight into the main entrance of town hall.

Annette fell back, her hand on her chest. "My goodness, Brody, you almost knocked me over."

Brody stepped into the entrance and tugged off his cowboy hat and Hannah felt that traitorous lift of her heart that accompanied thoughts of Brody.

"Sorry, ma'am. In a bit of a hurry," she heard Brody say.

"Then I'll let you get to it," Annette said.

Brody waited until the door fell shut behind Annette, then he strode over to the counter, his smile fading away as his booted feet echoed in the large atrium of the town hall. He wasn't smiling as he had last week when he'd come here, which managed to ease the silly beatings of her lonely heart.

"And what can I do for you, Mr. Harcourt?" she asked.

"So we're back to that again?" he said, his tone serious.

She shrugged, pleased that she could hold his gaze. Not so pleased that she still felt that unwelcome flutter in her heart.

Forget about it, Hannah reminded herself, glancing at the picture of the twins she had sitting on one corner of her desk. Beside it was a picture of David in his dress uniform.

Seeing David's picture was a gentle reminder and she pushed down her reaction to Brody, then turned back to him. "So what can I do for you?"

"Those your kids?" Brody asked, pointing to the picture beside her computer.

"Yes. Chrissy and Corey."

"Cute little munchkins. They must keep you busy."

His comment made her smile. "They do. But my parents help out a lot. My mother babysits every day I work."

Brody straightened, his hands resting on the counter. "Nice picture of David," he said, effectively bringing her deceased husband into the moment, as well.

David looked back at her, his expression serious, his dress uniform emphasizing his broad shoulders. She had gotten it only a few days ago from David's mother. In memory of David's birthday, she had told Hannah, giving her a hug of sympathy.

Hannah had placed it on the desk, though every time she looked at it, David's eyes seemed sadder and sadder.

"Anyway, I came to check to see if you got us that corner booth like we talked about last week?"

Hannah nodded. "I managed to talk the vet clinic into moving and they were happy to oblige once they knew the fire department was taking that space." She gave him a careful smile. "They figured it would only enhance their traffic."

"I hope so." Brody scratched the side of his head with a forefinger as if trying to draw out his next words. "Other reason I came was to talk about the job the committee wants us to take care of," Brody said, all crisp, discreet and businesslike. "How do you think we should deal with Lilibeth?"

"I'm not sure. Do you have any ideas?"

Brody leaned his elbows on the counter, which only served to bring him closer to her.

"I'm no detective, but I'm guessing we can start with talking to her, see if she knows anything."

"Which would give you the perfect opportunity to do what Abigail suggested?" Hannah asked, the faintly teasing comment slipping out of her.

Brody's eyes cut to her and then a lazy smile curved his mouth. "You mocking me, Mrs. Douglas?"

Why had she given in to the impulse? Once upon a time she'd had a sense of humor. She hadn't had much opportunity to use it for a while. But something about Brody seemed to tease it out of her.

"She might be a tough nut to crack," Hannah continued. "You could be like the…" She struggled to dredge up the term. Then she snapped her finger. "I know, the honey trap."

Brody's smile deepened, which only served to make

him look more attractive. "Thanks for your confidence in my abilities. I think I'll stick with questions and answers."

Their eyes held a heartbeat longer than necessary and Hannah felt as if her chest was constricting. She yanked her attention back to the matter at hand. "Sure. We can do that. Meantime, I could try to find out more about the Miss Jasper Gulch contest. That might be a good reason to take her out. Tell her what I know."

"Sounds like a good plan." Brody nodded as he turned his cowboy hat around in his hands. "Why don't you make the arrangements and let me know. Things will be picking up on the ranch in a couple of weeks, so the sooner the better."

"Sure. I'll call you."

"Do you have my cell phone number?"

"No. I should get that from you." She pulled out her cell phone and they exchanged numbers.

As she looked up at him, Brody's smile faded and she wondered if he was upset with her teasing. "Just want to say I'm sorry," he said quietly. "About the committee pushing us together like this."

His apology was sincere and acknowledged a simple fact. So why did it make her feel sad?

"It's okay. I can see why they want you to talk to Lilibeth. She does seem attracted to you and she'll probably open up quicker to you than anyone else."

"She's just a kid," Brody protested.

The door opened again and this time Mayor Shaw strode into the entrance. He wore a Western-cut suit jacket today, which, combined with his white shirt and black Stetson, gave him a commanding look. Usually he had a smile for Hannah, but today he looked especially grim.

His steps slowed when he saw Brody standing by Hannah's desk.

"Afternoon, Harcourt," Jackson Shaw said, stopping by the counter, his steely gaze ticking from Hannah to Brody. "How are things with you?" he asked, his deep voice smooth as any good politician's should be.

"Fine, just fine," Brody answered.

"Good year on the ranch?"

"We had a decent year. Only had a loss ratio of two percent, which we've never seen before," Brody said, straightening as he spoke to the mayor.

Hannah didn't blame him. Jackson Shaw was an imposing figure as well as a patriarch of the community. His ancestors were one of the two founding families of Jasper Gulch, the Shaws and the Masseys, and the only one to still have holdings in the area. Rather large holdings, too.

"That's good. Better than we did at our outfit. You raise Angus, correct?"

"Red Angus."

"Good breed. Thrifty calves. So, what brings you to town hall today?" Jackson's mouth shifted as he looked from Brody to Hannah. "You're not flirting with my secretary, are you?"

"Hannah and I are simply dealing with some time capsule business," Brody said.

Jackson Shaw's eyes narrowed. "She's had a tough go, Book-it Brody. David was a good man. They don't make many like him. He was a hero."

Brody straightened, and his mouth became tight at Mayor Shaw's not-so-subtle chiding and the use of his nickname. Hannah didn't blame him. Though he hadn't come out and said it, Mayor Shaw had inferred that Brody was in fact flirting with Hannah and was no match for David. Did Mayor Shaw see Brody as unsuitable?

You thought the same thing.

Mayor Shaw looked at Brody a moment longer, as if to underline what he'd said, then turned to Hannah. "How are things coming with the fair? Will we be able to fill the space?"

Hannah was surprised to see how quickly his expression shifted from stern to kind. How his features softened when he looked at her. It was as if he had pulled a mask off.

She couldn't identify what about that bothered her. It was as if he was a different person depending on who he was talking to. "We have most of the spaces for booths spoken for," she said. "The way things are going, I'm hoping we'll be all booked up by the end of the week." She hesitated a moment but felt she should say something on Brody's behalf to Mayor Shaw. "In fact, Brody booked two booths for the firefighters," she said. "And they hope to have their truck available for the children, which I'm excited about."

Mayor Shaw nodded, shot another quick look at Brody, as if still assessing his character, then turned his attention back to Hannah. "Did you confirm plans with the company who will be doing the midway?"

"Yes. We'll be having a carousel for the kids as well as a few other rides and a midway. We have them booked for the entire weekend."

"Perfect. Really good." He ran his hand over his hair and caught his lip between his teeth. Then without another word, he spun on his heel and with long, swinging strides walked away.

Brody blew out his breath as Jackson turned the corner and disappeared from view. Then he turned to Hannah. "Am I being oversensitive or did he seem kind of wound up?"

"He's been under a lot of pressure lately. It seems half the town wants us to use the money from the fundraisers for the museum we had planned for years, and the other half wants to use it to fix up the bridge over Beaver Creek, though Mayor Shaw prefers not to." She sighed as she looked up at Brody. "I'm surprised he remembered your nickname."

Brody slapped his cowboy hat against one leg. "I've had a few run-ins with him. I had his son Austin with me in the truck a couple of times when I got stopped by Deputy Calloway when we were in high school. Mayor Shaw collared me in the café and told me to stay away from his kid. Said I was a bad influence on him." Brody paused a moment, then seemed to shrug it off. "That was in the past, but he can't seem to let go. And, like Cord said, I don't go where I'm not wanted, so I tend to avoid him if I can."

"This time capsule theft has weighed heavy on his mind," Hannah said in Mayor Shaw's defense.

"It's just a capsule. I'm sure there's some neat memorabilia in it, but what could be in that capsule that losing it would make him so uptight?"

"I think he feels the pressure of his legacy. After all, Shaws have been a part of this community since it was founded. Maybe he feels like he's let that legacy down, especially after the whole fiasco was televised."

"I'm sure he feels foolish about it, but then again, he's not the one who stole it," Brody said with a laugh.

Hannah smiled at his joke. "No, but I know it bothers him."

"Which gives us more reason to talk to Lilibeth. L.S., to be precise," Brody said. "So if you can come with a few crumbs to give her from the minutes of the meetings, maybe we can get her to talk."

"Or you could turn on that Harcourt charm?" Hannah said with a teasing grin.

Brody pointed a finger at her. "Don't you start."

Hannah's grin widened, but she resisted the urge to make another quip.

He looked as if he wanted to say something more, then his gaze ticked over to David's picture and he dropped his hat on his head, turned and walked away.

Hannah released a careful sigh as she watched him go with a feeling of regret. For a moment, just a brief moment, she'd felt like a woman. Not a mother of two children and the widow of a hero.

She looked back at David's picture and made a face. "You put me in a real bind when you proposed just before you shipped out." But no sooner did she speak the words than she felt the usual guilt that seemed woven through her memories of David.

Yes, she had loved David, but in the weeks leading up to their wedding there were times that she wished she could slow everything down. Step back. Take a breath.

But she had agreed to everything David had wanted because she loved him and he was a soldier going to fight for his country. She had agreed to the bare-bones civil ceremony with only Julie and his friend as attendants. Had agreed to the simple honeymoon in Bozeman at a bed-and-breakfast.

And then in a matter of heartbeats it was over. David had shipped out and she was left wondering if the wedding had happened at all.

Hannah sloughed off those pointless thoughts. Regardless of how it came about, she had married David and now was his widow raising his twins. This was her reality. She just had to go with what life brought her.

Brody drummed his fingers on the table of the booth at the back of the café. He wished, for the fifth time since he'd come here, that he hadn't agreed to this meeting with Hannah and Lilibeth. First off, the whole idea that Lilibeth Shoemaker had anything to do with the time capsule theft was crazy. Sure she was upset, but she didn't seem that vindictive. Second, meeting with Hannah was also not a good idea. He was having such conflicting thoughts about the girl. On the one hand, he was attracted to her. On the other, he thought of the complications that were a part of her life. Widow of a hero. Mother of twins.

The door of the café opened again and Hannah stepped inside. Her plain white T-shirt was enhanced by a cluster of silver dangly necklaces, fitted blue jeans and large black purse that gave her a simple but classy look.

He sighed, crossing his arms over his chest as Hannah walked toward him. She gave him a careful smile and then slipped into the seat across from him.

"Lilibeth not here yet?"

"Not yet."

Hannah set her purse to one side and pulled out a file folder and set it on the table. "I managed to glean a few things from the minutes I thought might interest Lilibeth."

"We're not breaking some privacy act with this?" Brody asked.

Hannah shook her head, a hank of dark hair falling across her cheek. She tucked it back, looking at the folder she was flipping through. "No. In fact, Mayor

Shaw read through the minutes himself to find what I might need. He thought I was too busy to do it myself."

"He's taking quite a personal interest in your involvement," Brody said. An edge of anger entered his voice when he thought of Mayor Shaw. The man's use of Brody's nickname the other day and his apparent protectiveness toward Hannah still irked him. As if Brody had no right to show any interest in the man's secretary.

"He knows I have a lot going on," Hannah said, sounding defensive. "He's been busy, so I really appreciated his taking time to help us with this."

"Of course he's busy," Brody said, hoping to assure her. He *was* being oversensitive and he knew it. "There's been a lot going on with the centennial and there'll be even more happening over the next few months."

"I just hope we can get this time capsule thing solved. I know it will take a huge load off his mind," Hannah said, folding her hands. She released a light sigh, tapping her thumbs together as she glanced at her watch, looking everywhere but at him. She clearly wanted to be somewhere else.

"Have you seen Lilibeth?" Hannah asked finally. "She wasn't working at the ice-cream parlor today."

"I came here right from the ranch."

Mert came with menus and set them on the table, then poured coffee for both of them. She raised one eyebrow, winked at Brody, then left. He stifled a sigh, guessing Mert's knowing look was a result of her promise to find him a wife the last time he'd been here.

But her wink and look made him suddenly overly aware of Hannah. And, even more disconcerting, suddenly tongue-tied. Brody liked to pride himself on being able to chat up women, but something about Hannah sucked all the smart out of him.

Hannah cleared her throat and looked as if she was about to break the awkward silence, when he heard the sound of someone clearing his throat.

Brody fought down a beat of frustration as he glanced over at Ethan Johnson standing beside them. He wore his usual blue jeans and a sweatshirt that was ragged at the cuffs. He certainly didn't look like a pastor.

"Hannah. Brody." Pastor Ethan's deep brown eyes flicked from one to the other as if assessing the situation. "Nice to see you two here."

"Oh, we're not together," Hannah said, cutting off anything Pastor Ethan might have to say with a quick wave of her hand, her comment and action extinguishing the faint spark of encouragement Brody had felt. "Brody and I are here only on time capsule business."

"Time capsule business," Ethan said, his smile growing. "Sounds official." He then reached into his back pocket. "I stopped at town hall but read your note that you would be here. I'm donating a basket to the auction. A food basket."

He set a completed application in front of Hannah.

"Really?" The surprised word came out before Brody could stop it.

"Don't sound so shocked," Ethan said, grinning at Brody. "Baking and cooking are manly occupations."

"I didn't say they weren't," Brody spluttered. "Just seems…interesting. Not something I would have associated with you."

"Actually, it was a dare from Cord Shaw," Ethan said. "We were talking about the basket auction and I asked him if he was going to bid on someone special's basket. He kind of sneered about it. Said there was no one special for him and he wasn't bidding on any basket unless it was to see if the person bidding was serious. So I told him if I donated a basket he had to bid. He laughed, agreed but said I wouldn't do it. So here I am. Proving him wrong." Ethan stood back and folded his arms over his chest, smiling down at Hannah.

"That's very generous of you."

"Maybe you could bid on it," Ethan suggested to Hannah.

Was that a twinkle in his eye? Brody wondered. And was Hannah actually toying with her hair? As if she was flirting with him?

Jealousy twinged through Brody. Ethan, a pastor, would be exactly the kind of person Hannah should be with. Good-looking. A good man and well respected in the community he'd joined only a few months ago.

Someone who could probably hold a candle to David's memory.

Brody clenched his hands under the table, wishing that didn't bother him as much as it did.

"Trouble is, I can't," Hannah said as Brody focused his attention on his coffee. "I'm organizing it, so I would know who made which basket and it is supposed to be a secret."

"Too bad," Ethan said, looking from Brody to Hannah, his faint smirk showing Brody that he didn't believe Hannah's quick protestations that she and Brody were not here together. "But I won't bother you anymore and shall leave you two alone."

And before either Hannah or Brody could correct his assumption, he turned and walked away, stopping at a table farther on to chat with Chauncey Hardman and Rosemary Middleton, who sat at their table with their tea and knitting.

Brody watched as Ethan smiled and chatted, charm personified. A good man.

Like David.

The kind of man Brody wasn't.

Chapter Four

Hannah shot a quick glance at her watch, then at the menus still sitting on their table. Everywhere but at the tall handsome man across from her.

He made her fidgety and she found herself far too aware of him.

"Lilibeth better show up quick or I'll have to grab something and run," she said finally, breaking the awkward silence that fell after Pastor Ethan left.

While she and Brody had been sitting here, she had seen four people come to the door of the town hall, read her note and walk on. If she went back to the office without eating now, chances were she wouldn't have an opportunity until the office was closed.

"Why don't we just order now," Brody said, picking up the menu. "Maybe Lilibeth will come soon."

"Mayor Shaw did say I could take a longer break than normal because I'm on town business," she said, feeling as if she had to justify her time here. "And I didn't have time to eat breakfast."

"Busy morning?" Brody asked.

"Chrissy has been a little bear. She's teething and doesn't want to settle down. I think she cried for an hour last night. I'm not sure what to do for her." Hannah stopped the flow of meaningless chatter. A single guy like Brody wouldn't be the least bit interested in the trials and tribulations of a single mother. She cleared her throat, picked up the menu and frowned at it, as if trying to decide what she wanted. She knew she should go with healthy but right now what she craved more than anything was a burger.

Finally Mert showed up, looking from Hannah to Brody. "You two lovebirds ready?"

Hannah was about to correct her when Brody spoke up.

"I'll have a quesadilla with sour cream and guacamole on the side and salad instead of fries," Brody said, folding his arms over his chest, staring at Mert as if he wanted to tell her something.

"Salad. How very healthy of you," Hannah said, glancing over at him.

He shifted his attention from Mert to her. "Cowboys got to keep up their strength."

"So what do you think you'll have, sweetie?" Mert asked as she refilled their coffee cups.

"I think I'll have a cheeseburger," she said.

"Not a very balanced meal," Brody said in a teasing tone. "Where are your vegetables?"

"You're right," she said, looking up at Mert. "Can you put onion rings with that?"

"Sure thing," she said, making a note on her pad.

"And how is that balanced?" Brody asked.

"Onions are a vegetable," Hannah said with fake innocence.

Brody's resulting laugh created a surprising uptick in her heart rate. And when he looked over at her, his grin still creasing his face, making a fan of wrinkles that framed his dark eyes, her breath seemed to leave her, as well.

She tore her gaze away, wishing Lilibeth would come to remind Hannah of the futility of becoming interested in someone like Brody Harcourt.

"You sure you don't want a salad?" Mert asked, sounding motherly. "You don't want to end up like poor Wes Middleton. Heart surgery ain't no picnic, though we're sure hoping he gets better soon. That wife of his does like to chitchat. Never seen the likes of it. Takes me longer to get groceries now that she's working there than it did when Wes was still around." Mert shook her head as she stuck her pencil behind her ear, tucked their menus under her arm and walked back to the counter to put their order in to Vincente.

"Interesting to hear the pot talking about the kettle," Hannah said with a wry expression after Mert was gone.

"Mert probably doesn't get much of a chance to speak her mind around Rosemary."

Her laugh gleaned her another grin from Brody. Their eyes met and once again Hannah felt her attention drifting toward him and away from the everyday cares that clung to her as his smile settled into her heart. Then he looked away, turning his attention to the folder on the table beside her, and she caught herself. A quick shake of her head brought her back to reality.

"What did you manage to find in the minutes that Lilibeth might be interested in?" Brody asked.

"Not a lot. Some behind-the-scenes information on the judging process and what they were looking for." Hannah tucked her hair behind her ear and flipped through the folder. "Since the queen was crowned at the rodeo, the judges were hoping to find someone with—" Hannah made little quote marks with her fingers

"'—high aptitude in equine prowess,' as the minutes put it."

"Equine prowess. Wow. Someone was really putting their thesaurus to work."

"Lilibeth seemed to lack in the equine prowess department, so I'm hoping that will help her understand why she didn't win."

"And then what?" Brody asked.

"What do you mean?"

"So after we tell her the reason she wasn't crowned Miss Jasper Gulch, how do we segue into finding out what she knows about the time capsule?"

"Segue? Someone else has been using his thesaurus," Hannah joked, surprised at how effortlessly he put her at ease. How being around him brought out a sense of humor that David didn't always appreciate.

"I may wear a cowboy hat and put out fires, but I do know my way around the English language," he returned, his own smile deepening. "I've always liked reading."

"Ms. Hardman at the library must have loved you."

"She tolerated me because I read. But we all know she's not too crazy about cowboys ever since her mother ran off with one," Brody said with a twinkle in his eye.

"Long time to hold a grudge," Hannah agreed, her silly heart doing a tiny flip at the way he held her eyes.

"Speaking of grudges," Brody said, leaning closer to her, lowering his voice, creating a sense of intimacy that gave her a tiny shiver. "Do you really think Lilibeth stole that time capsule?"

Hannah cupped her mug of coffee, running her finger down the side, slowly shaking her head as she tried to imagine someone as slight as Lilibeth handling something the size and weight of the time capsule. "I can't think of why she would want to do it. Nor can I imagine her doing all that hard work," she said.

"Unless she had an accomplice so she could save her manicure," Brody said with another grin.

"Lilibeth may come across as shallow," she said, feeling a need to defend the young girl, "but I believe she has a good heart. At any rate, her stealing the time capsule doesn't seem plausible. She couldn't have had a reason to do it. I just wonder who could have done it and why?"

"Lilibeth is our only lead, if we want to believe she's the L.S in the note Cord got. We haven't found anyone else in town with the initials L.S. And if she doesn't show up today, we might have to reschedule."

"I don't know if I'll have time to meet her again. I've got a lot going on right now."

Brody folded his arms on the table, still leaning forward. "I imagine your twins keep you busy, as well."

Hannah's smile tightened, his words a reminder of her responsibilities. "They do keep me busy. But I love them to bits."

"I'm sure. It must be nice for your parents to have you and the kids close."

"They love it, but I think it's wearing on my mother. Because of the centennial celebrations, I've been working longer hours and my mother's been taking care of the kids for me. She's doesn't have as much energy as she used to and the twins can be a real handful."

"I can't imagine taking care of two kids the same age. And all by yourself."

"It has its challenges," she said quietly, wishing, for a fleeting moment, that he hadn't brought up the twins. For a few fleeting moments she had felt like a woman, not a weary, widowed mother of two children.

She took a sip of water then set the cup down. "And what about you? You seem to have your own challenges to deal with. Firefighting? Ranching? That must keep you busy, as well."

"At times."

"So what made you take up firefighting?"

"The challenge, I guess. I wanted to do something more than just ranch, plus it was a way of helping out."

"And the adventure."

Brody shrugged. "Partly. I like the feeling that I'm contributing to the community. Giving back, so to speak."

"By saving Alfie Hart's dog?" She couldn't help bringing up the conversation she had overheard the last time she'd sat in this café. The thought of him willing to run into a burning building made her realize how risky Brody's job was. "Would you have gone in?"

"I had a mask and all my gear on. The fire wasn't critical yet. The structure was still sound." He sounded so casual about it. As if going into a burning building was no big deal. "Besides, I'm the one with the most training, so I'm often first man in on a fire."

"Sounds dangerous." She grew serious as she looked down at her glass and sighed lightly, thinking of David so willing to join the army. So willing to jump into the fray, just as Brody seemed to be. David said it was to serve his country, but whenever he talked about his training and about possibly going overseas, she caught a gleam in his eye she had never seen in all the times they were dating. He talked about adventure as much as he talked about serving. If he hadn't enlisted—

She stopped her thoughts there. She couldn't indulge in might-have-beens. It was this practicality that got her through David's death and the discovery that she would have to raise twins on her own. "You men seem drawn to that kind of thing," she said, unable to keep the rueful tone out of her voice.

"It's a job that needs to be done. But that's the reality." He angled his head as if to study her better. "But enough about me. What about you? What made you decide to work at the town hall? You've been there since high school, haven't you?"

She nodded. "I started when I was a sophomore. I liked office work, and when the job came up I took it. When David and I graduated, I started working full-time. I only worked part-time after the twins were born, but since the centennial business started, I've been full-time again."

"Did you ever want to do anything different? Go somewhere else?"

She tested that thought a moment, wondering if he would understand her answer. "I've thought of traveling many times. David and I talked about seeing New York City. Paris. Athens. But he's gone and I've got the kids now, so I won't be going anywhere for a while."

"You could travel once they get older," Brody said. "It's not completely out of the question."

"Where would you go if you could travel?"

Brody's smile softened. "I always wanted to buy an old camper, drop it on my truck and visit every state on the mainland."

"That would be fun. Where would you go first?"

"Idaho. It's the closest. Then Washington State. Then Oregon. After that, it gets tricky. But I had a plan." Brody pulled a pen out of his pocket and grabbed a napkin and soon was showing Hannah the route he would take that would get him through all the states with the shortest distance traveled.

Hannah was intrigued by his plan and had to laugh at some of the detours he wanted to make.

"Hannah. There you are," a voice called out across the café.

Hannah's heart faltered as she looked away from Brody's intricate mapping in time to see her mother-in-law, Allison Douglas, walking toward her. She wore a blue-and-white-striped shirt, blue pants and a white sweater with the sleeves tied over her shoulders and an oversize leather handbag slung over her shoulder. Her hair was perfect. Her makeup perfect. She wore a pearl necklace and pearl earrings. Every time Hannah saw her she had to fight the urge to look down at her own clothes and make sure they were free of stains and un-wrinkled. Which they never were.

"I thought you might be here when I saw the sign on the door of the town office." Allison laid her hand on Hannah's arm, her eyes holding their perpetual look of sympathy each time she saw Hannah. She eased out a melancholy sigh, then turned to Brody, and for some reason her smile stiffened.

"Brody Harcourt," she said, acknowledging him with a tight nod of her perfectly colored and cut blond hair, her voice suddenly chilled.

"Do you want to join us, Mrs. Douglas?" Hannah asked.

Allison looked at Brody a moment longer, then turned back to her, her smile shifting so quickly Han-nah thought she had imagined the momentary chill. "No. I can see you are busy with this man," she said with a dismissive wave of her hand toward Brody. "I'm sorry I'm interrupting."

And Hannah suddenly understood the reason for her mother-in-law's frosty attitude toward Brody. She thought they were on a date. She wanted to correct that assumption, but before she could say anything, Allison was speaking again.

"But while I'm here, I may as well give you this." She unzipped her bag. "I was doing some fall cleaning when I found something I thought you might be interested in. I forgot to give it to you the last time you came to visit with the twins." She pulled out a large envelope that had Hannah's name written on it in a flowing script. Her smile grew sorrowful as she set it on the table and patted it gently. "These are some letters that you sent David while he was in training. He brought them back home before you got married." Her voice wavered a moment and once again Hannah was overcome with sympathy for her mother-in-law.

"Thank you," she said quietly, touching the envelope. "I appreciate that."

"I know David treasured every letter he received from you," Mrs. Douglas whispered, her voice choked. "But it didn't seem right for me to keep them." She patted Hannah on the shoulder and looked from her to the envelope as if she expected Hannah would jump on them. "I knew how special they would be for you. You and David had a one-of-a-kind relationship."

"Thank you for them," Hannah said, folding her hands on the table. She sensed that Mrs. Douglas wanted her to open them right away, but Hannah wasn't ready to face that.

Mrs. Douglas looked disappointed at Hannah's muted reaction. "I also wanted to tell you that Sam and I are leaving Monday on a ten-day cruise," she continued. "We're finally going to Alaska. David had always encouraged us to go. I think we should."

"I think you should, too, and if I don't see you on

Sunday, I hope you have a wonderful time," Hannah said, giving her mother-in-law what she hoped was an encouraging smile.

"You won't be coming to church again?"

It was the "again" that raised the usual pangs of conscience that Hannah felt each time Sunday morning came around and the thought of dealing with her twins during the church service made her stay at home.

"I don't know. The last time I attended, the twins were awful." Hannah had come to church, but she was tired, the twins were cranky and she'd had to make an embarrassingly emotional exit.

"You could try one more time," Allison suggested.

"Maybe. We'll see."

"Anyhow, you take care, my dear, and if we don't see you Sunday, maybe we'll stop at the apartment to say goodbye?"

Hannah mentally compared her perpetually untidy apartment to Allison's immaculate home and suppressed a shudder. The last time she had visited, Corey had left handprints all over the window and Allison had followed him around, cleaning up behind him. Meeting her at church might be a better option. "Maybe I'll try church again," she said quickly.

"That would be nice," Allison said. She glanced sidelong at Brody as if surprised he was still there, then turned and walked away. Before she left the café, however, she shot another look over her shoulder at Hannah. Hannah gave her a little wave and when the door closed, leaned back and released her breath. Allison was a good, kind person, but she always made Hannah feel nervous and uptight.

Brody looked as if he was about to say something, but just then Mert came with their food. Hannah moved the envelope holding her letters to David aside to make room. But for the rest of the meal, she sensed them lying there, bringing David's presence back into the moment.

Brody parked his truck in the parking lot of the church, looking forward to the switch in direction that the service would give his thoughts.

Ever since Friday, when he'd had lunch with Hannah, he couldn't keep her off his mind. Trouble was, he'd been equally unable to keep David off his mind.

When Mrs. Douglas brought those letters to the café, it was like another blow to his attraction to Hannah. She looked so sad and heartbroken as she took the envelope from Mrs. Douglas. In that moment, though part of him had clung to a faint hope, he was clearly shown he could never compete with that man's memory. He could not replace David in her life.

It also didn't help that Mrs. Douglas had her own memories of Brody. Too easily he recalled sitting in the school office, sent there for yet another offense. Mrs. Douglas was the school secretary and the disapproving looks she sent him those times were much like the ones he got from her the other day in the café.

It was as if to tell him something he already knew. He could never replace David in Hannah's life. He would never be good enough.

Brody fought down a moment of despair.

Help me, Lord, he prayed. *Help me to know that my first priority is to love and serve You. To find my completeness in You and not in being married and having a partner.*

He paused a moment, as if to let the prayer bind itself to his life, to let the peace he prayed for settle into his soul.

Then he got out of the truck just as his father and mother pulled up beside him.

"I didn't think we'd catch up to you," his mother said as she stepped out of the truck.

"I took the long way around. Needed to think."

His mother shot him a piercing look, as if trying to ferret out why he might need to do that, but he just tucked his keys in the pocket of his pants and gave her a bland smile.

"Didn't have a chance to talk to you this morning," his dad said. "We're going to have to move those cows this week."

"Really, Winston, do you have to talk business on the Lord's Day?" Brody's mother asked, sounding a bit peeved.

"All work done for the glory of God is worthy to be discussed on the Sabbath," his father returned with a gracious smile.

She harrumphed as they walked toward the front entrance, glancing at her watch as she stopped there. "It's later than I thought." She looked over at Brody. "Your father and I have to go to the parish office and pick up books for our Bible study, so could you go to the kitchen and pick up my salad bowl? The glass one with the leaves etched on it, and could you bring it back to the truck? I promised Annette Lakey she could borrow it for a party she's throwing for her husband, Tony, and she was going to get it out of our truck this morning."

"Sure thing," he said, and made the turn to the left while his mother and father went to the right. His booted feet echoed on the wooden ramp beside the main church building leading to the wings off the back of the sanctuary. He pulled the door of the building open and the first thing he heard was the sound of a child's screams.

The nursery was directly ahead of him, but the sound was coming from the end of the hallway to his left. He turned and was surprised to see Hannah holding the hand of her little boy, who was pulling away from her while she tried to cuddle a very upset little girl.

Hannah wore a dress today in a pale shade of pink that shimmered and flowed around her legs as she crouched down to set the crying girl on her feet on the floor.

"Honey. It's okay. You don't have to go to the nursery. You can stay with Mommy," Brody heard her saying as she brushed a fluff of blond curls away from the little girl's chubby tear-stained face. The little girl, still sobbing, had grabbed at her dress, the same shade of pink as her mother's, and was twisting it in her hands. "It's okay, honey. It's church. You want to go to church, don't you?" Hannah stroked her face, then shot a quick look at the boy, still leaning away from her in a silent tug-of-war. He wore a white shirt, a tiny bow tie, sagging shorts and a look of dogged determination.

Brody guessed he didn't want to go to church, either.

"Everything okay?" he asked, though clearly it wasn't.

Hannah spun around and, as she did, the little boy gained his freedom. He would have crashed to the floor, but Brody snagged him around the middle and hiked him onto his hip.

The little girl stopped her crying, sneaking a peek past Hannah as if to see who this strange person was.

Hannah lifted her up as she turned toward Brody.

Surprise jolted through him. Her hair was curled, half of it pulled back from her face by a gold clip. She wore a gold necklace that matched the rows of tiny gold sparkles on the pleats at the top of her shimmery pink dress. She looked almost ethereal and untouchable.

"Hi. Sorry about that." Her apology was breathless and hurried as she bent over to pick up a large bag from the floor. "I thought I would try to take the kids in church today because last time I was here I had to make the march up the front of the church to the nursery in the middle of the service because I could hear the kids crying. Just wailing they were so upset. Then I thought they would settle with me, but of course they didn't and I ended up walking out of church with them anyway. I thought I would try again today." Hannah shifted the bag onto her shoulder and gave him an apologetic look. "And I'm stopping now."

"So this is Corey?" Brody asked, looking down at the little boy in his arms. His hair wasn't as long as his sister's, but it curled over his ears. Large brown eyes stared back at him, showing no emotion.

"Yes. And this is Chrissy." Hannah dropped a quick kiss of consolation on the little girl's forehead. "My drama queen."

"Can I help?"

Hannah waved off his offer so fast he almost felt insulted. "Thank you, but my parents said they would help me today. I thought I would first see if the twins would go into the nursery." She released a wry laugh. "Obviously that was a bust."

"Where were you going to meet your parents?"

"At the back of the church," she said, reaching out to take Corey from him.

"I can bring him for you." The little guy was heavy. He couldn't imagine her carrying both of the kids around. Especially the way Corey squirmed.

Hannah looked a if she was about to protest again,

but then her shoulders drooped just a little and she accepted his help with a smile. "Thanks. That would be great." She adjusted her purse and looked as if she was about to say more, when something or someone behind him caught her attention.

Brody turned in time to see his mother coming down the hallway from the office, his father right behind her.

"Brody, did you find that bowl?" she was asking.

"No. Haven't got there yet."

"Winston, would you mind getting the bowl and putting it in the truck?"

Without a word, his father went to the kitchen.

Gina turned, looking from Hannah to Brody, her smile deepening. "Hello, Hannah. How are you doing?"

"Busy. Had a minor crisis here, but then Brody helped out."

"I see that." She tucked her hair behind her ear and touched Corey on the shoulder. "Aren't you a little munchkin?" she said. "All dressed up in your Sunday best."

"Look at the cute bow tie," Brody said, pointing it out to his mother.

"Oh, my goodness. He's adorable."

Brody felt a tiny twinge at the softened tone of his mother's voice and the way her features melted at the sight of the children. Wasn't hard to hear the faint yearning in her voice. She gave him a careful smile as she glanced from Hannah back to him again, a question in her eyes.

Not this girl, he wanted to tell her.

"So, were you going to put the twins in the nursery?" she asked Hannah.

"Um. No. I… Uh…I have to have them in church."

"Separation anxiety?" his mother asked in a sympathetic voice. "I understand. My one daughter hated the nursery and as a result Sunday was never that day of rest I was always promised." His mother held out her hands as if to take Corey from Brody and with a reluctance that surprised him, Brody handed him over.

Didn't anyone think he was capable of taking care of a little boy?

"You are so cute," his mother said, reverting to the baby-talk voice that always took over whenever she was around little children.

"Maybe we should go back to the entrance?" Hannah asked. "The kids seem to be settled down and I don't want my parents to miss me."

Brody held the door open as first Hannah and then his mother walked through. He followed behind, unable to keep his eyes off Hannah, holding her little girl, her dark hair glistening in the sun, swinging as she walked.

And stop, he told himself as they turned toward the foyer. He hurried ahead and held the door open again.

No sooner had they entered the foyer than there was her father, pacing back and forth in the entrance. He shoved his hand through his thinning hair, hiked up a pair of pants that looked too large for him and buttoned up his tweed blazer as he looked over the people moving through the foyer of the church toward the entrance to the sanctuary. Rosemary Middleton bustled up to him before they could get to him and grabbed him by the arm, her head bobbing in greeting. "Gregory. I heard Lori is under the weather. How is she today?"

Her father blinked as if confused, and Hannah looked equally perplexed as she walked over to her father, Brody and his mother in tow. "Dad? What is Mrs. Middleton talking about?"

Her father's head snapped from Rosemary to his

daughter and his features seemed to collapse. "Oh, honey. I'm so sorry. I was looking for you to tell you myself. She—"

"Your mother is doing very poorly," Rosemary cut off her father's explanation, folding her arms over her ample midsection. She wore a blue-striped dress that looked as if it would have fit her better twenty pounds ago. "I overheard Jane Franklin saying that she saw Lori coming out of the clinic on Friday, looking like death warmed over."

"Friday? But Mom was watching the twins for me that day," Hannah said, sounding agitated. "I know she was tired. I didn't think she was sick."

"Could have been Saturday, too," Rosemary mused, tapping her finger on her chin. "Come to think of it, I am sure it was Saturday, not Friday, because the produce truck didn't come Friday and I had to put out some new magazines. Yes. Probably Saturday."

Brody tried not to smile at Rosemary's meddling, but he felt bad for Hannah's distress at the thought that her mother was taking care of her children while sick.

"Why didn't Mom say anything when I talked to her yesterday?" Hannah continued.

Her father pulled out a handkerchief and patted his forehead, looking as troubled as Hannah sounded. "Well, now, she wasn't that bad on Friday. It got worse that night. Bad cough and feeling run-down. She's in bed now. She probably won't be able to take the kids for a couple of days. The doctor was worried it might be pneumonia. Said she should rest for at least three or four days. Maybe more. I don't know."

Hannah bit her lip at her father's distress as she pulled Chrissy closer. "Can I do anything for her?"

Her father patted her on the shoulder. "Honey, you've

got enough and I'm more than capable of taking care of her. You just worry about the kids."

"Okay. So I'll have to call Aunt Mathilda to babysit."

"I think she's out of town," her father said.

"Maybe I could call Julie—"

"I could watch them," Brody's mother put in so quickly it was as if she was waiting for exactly this opportunity.

Brody shot a puzzled glance at his mother. What was she doing?

She elbowed him. Gently, mind you, but still an elbow, and added a reproving look. Then she turned to Hannah, smile firmly in place. "I know how hard it will be to find someone on such short notice and I also know how busy you are at town hall. So I'm more than willing to come and pick up the children and bring them to the ranch to watch them for you. If that's okay?"

"You are an angel in disguise, helping out this poor young widow and her children." Rosemary turned to Hannah and touched her shoulder. "That will be a real support to you, and that way your mother doesn't have to worry herself about not being able to help you out. I'm sure that will be a huge load off her shoulders. I know my Wes feels so much better knowing that I'm keeping the store going while he recuperates from his surgery. This is a fantastic idea." Then she trundled off, looking as satisfied as if she had personally volunteered to help Hannah out.

Brody felt his heart sink. Bad enough he was on the Time Capsule Committee with Hannah, he didn't know how he was going to handle seeing her every day at his own home. Being reminded every day of how improbable it was for him to be a part of her life.

"I'm sorry I can't stay," her father was saying. "I've

got to go back to help your mother. I won't be able to help you with the twins during the service, but I'm so thankful that Mrs. Harcourt can." He gave Brody's mother a tight nod, then turned back to Hannah. "Your mother will be so relieved to know that."

Hannah bit her lip and Brody could see she was torn.

"And we'll lend a hand this morning," his mother said.

"I'm not sure how it will go." Hannah held Chrissy close. "I haven't been able to attend an entire service since the twins were born."

Her comment tore at Brody's soul. He knew how much he needed church. He also knew that she didn't attend much. He had mistakenly assumed it was because she didn't want to. That she couldn't hadn't crossed his mind.

"I think between you, me and my parents, we can figure something out," Brody said.

She looked over at him and he could see the tension in her shoulders ease. "That would be nice" was all she said.

And as they all walked into church together, Brody felt as if his life was shifting into a different place.

Did he dare go there?

Chapter Five

❧

"So, it must have been nice to be in church again yesterday," Julie said, following Hannah to one of the picnic tables set up by the concession booth of the fairgrounds.

"It was really nice," Hannah replied as she unrolled her main plan for the fairgrounds, anchoring it with her purse on one side, her cell phone on the other. "And now Mrs. Harcourt is taking care of the kids."

Hannah shot a quick glance at her phone, wondering if she should text Brody's mother and see how the kids were doing. Mrs. Harcourt had sent her a couple of texts and pictures this morning to let her know the kids were fine.

But the last one had come more than a couple of hours ago and Hannah wondered how Brody's mom was coping.

"And sitting with the Harcourts in church? How did that happen?"

"They offered their help," Hannah said, Julie's teasing tone pulling her attention away from the phone. "Dad had to go home to take care of Mom, so I accepted. Simple as that."

However, it wasn't simple as that once she sat down in the pew beside Brody. Too easily she recalled how she'd felt sitting beside him in church. How he had held the songbook open for her as she held Chrissy. David would do that for her, and as she followed along, standing beside Brody, holding David's child, Hannah had felt a mixture of sorrow and guilt. She knew she was becoming attracted to Brody, but she wasn't sure what to make of her changing feelings.

"So. How do you think we lay this out?" Hannah asked, changing the topic. She tucked her hair behind her ear as she looked from the plans laid in front of her to the fairgrounds, which suddenly seemed too small for everything they needed to put there.

This morning, Mayor Shaw had asked her to pace out the layout of the booths and make sure there was enough space at the fairgrounds. Hannah had sent out a desperate appeal to her friend Julie for her help. Thankfully, Julie managed to rope in her fiancé, Ryan, who, with Julie's brother Cord, was now measuring out the potential layout of the booths and the midway.

"According to the midway people, they'll need at least half of the available space," Hannah continued, looking from the plans to grounds edged by the river on one side and, on the other, a grove of cottonwoods with a number of old buildings left over from one of the earlier settlers who had sold out to the town years ago.

"I sure wish those old Shoemaker barns were gone. That would give us space," Julie said.

"Trust me, if we try to do something about them, Lilibeth might complain about it being a historical site. That was her grandparents' old place, after all, and she's still fussing about not being chosen Miss Jasper Gulch. So we'll have to work with the space we've got."

"So start turning people down for booths. No sense in making yourself crazy and cramming everyone in. I know I want people to be able to walk around my booth and see all my wool and knitted goods. If you put too many side by side it will be too cramped."

Julie had been one of the first people to book a booth for her wool business. Hannah and her children had been the happy recipients of many colorful hand-knit sweaters made from wool Julie had sheared from her own sheep.

"I'll have to. Besides, we're getting down to the wire."

Julie tapped her pencil against her chin as she scanned Hannah's master plan. "We could cut some down. How about the firefighters? Since when do they need two booths?"

"Brody asked for two so they could have room to park their truck behind it for the kids. I thought it was a great idea. Besides, they're volunteers who put their lives on the line. I don't want to deny them what they asked for."

"Of course. Sure." Julie gave her a baffled look, which made Hannah realize how defensive she sounded. "I just thought if we need more room, that was a place to start."

Hannah didn't reply, realizing that her reaction to Julie's suggestion was a mixture of the confusion she felt around Brody and the tension she'd been feeling all morning. When Mrs. Harcourt had come this morning to pick up the children, Brody had come, as well. Seeing him holding Chrissy, looking so at ease with the twins, had created a blend of melancholy and a curious sense of appeal that had only been kindled by sitting beside him in church yesterday.

Melancholy for the fact that David hadn't even known about his children and would never see them.

Appeal for the man that had, of late, been slowly taking up more and more of her mental space. And she wasn't sure how to feel about the mixture of emotions she felt each time she saw him.

She shot another look at her phone. In half an hour she had to leave to pick up the kids.

And see Brody again.

"That's the fourth time you've done that in the past half hour," Julie said, nudging her friend with an elbow and faking a look of hurt. "I'm starting to think you don't want to be here. You in a hurry to get home?"

"I'm feeling a bit stressed about the kids. I know they're fine. It's just, it feels like they're so far away. I'm used to knowing I can just pop across the street if I needed to."

"Harcourt ranch isn't that far out of town. But, hey, if it will make you feel better to see them, just go. I can cover for you here."

"But your dad wanted to see the layout this afternoon."

No sooner had she spoken than a truck pulled into the parking lot and Jackson Shaw got out. He was frowning as he strode toward Hannah and Julie.

"How are things coming?" he asked as he came up beside them, glancing from where Ryan and his son Cord were working to Julie and Hannah. "Is this going to come together? Will you have enough room?"

"Everything is fine, Dad," Julie said, giving him a quick smile. "Ryan is being a real help."

"Did you and Harcourt have a chance to talk to Lilibeth yet?" Jackson asked Hannah. "About the time capsule?"

"We were supposed to meet her, but she didn't show."

"That sounds suspicious," Mayor Shaw said. "Maybe I should go have a talk with her."

Julie laid her hand on her father's arm. "You're busy enough, Dad. Let the committee take care of it."

"We need to get this resolved."

"Of course we do," Hannah assured him. "I'll talk to Brody next time I see him about meeting with Lilibeth again." Hannah fought down a beat of panic as she thought of all the things that needed to be done before the fair began. And now her mother was sick and somehow she had to find the time to see her, as well.

Just then Cord and Ryan joined them, holding out a piece of paper with a number of figures written down. "As long as nothing changes and you don't get more booths, you'll have enough space," Cord said.

Hannah was about to take it from him, when Julie intercepted. "Me and the guys will lay this all out."

"But you need to make sure—"

"We've got it," Julie said, waving her off. "Now go and get your kids."

Hannah glanced at Mayor Shaw, who was technically her boss, but he was talking to Cord and Ryan, all three of them now bent over the master plan Hannah had drawn up.

"Thanks. I'll see you tomorrow," she said, then turned and hurried to her car.

The tension of the day seemed to pile on her as she headed up Shaw Boulevard and then out toward the Harcourt ranch. All the way there she tried not to speed. Tried not to let the worry that had hung at the back of her mind make her rush. In spite of the texts and the constant assurance that the kids were fine, Hannah had felt a curious vulnerability over the children and being so far from them.

Hannah slowed as she approached the entrance to the ranch, then drove up the driveway.

The first thing she saw was a grouping of buildings made up of a large barn, hay sheds and, situated against a line of trees, a log house with a veranda that overlooked the valley sweeping away from the ranch toward the mountains beyond.

A truck was parked in front of the house. Mrs. Harcourt had come with an SUV, but Hannah couldn't see it.

Don't panic, she told herself as she slowed, still following the driveway that went past the house and over a hill.

She crested the hill and then saw what she suspected was the main house, Gina's SUV parked in the driveway in front of it. The house was finished with stucco and brick, creating a look of warmth and elegance at the same time. As she drove closer, she noticed the flower beds tucked up against the house and along the edge of a brick path leading to a large wooden door framed by sidelights and an arched window above the door. The door had bay windows on each side. Beyond the house the land seemed to drop away into a valley guarded by the mountains.

She parked her car and slowly got out, suddenly feeling somewhat intimidated by the beautiful home, trying to imagine her children riding roughshod through a home even more elegant than her in-laws'.

She unzipped her purse and was about to pull out a tube of lipstick to freshen up, when a brown-and-white dog came gamboling around the back of the house, plumed tail wagging, tongue hanging out, pointy ears perked up as it barked a welcome. It danced around her and she laughed. "You look like Cowboy Dan," she said, thinking of her friend Julie's Australian shepherd dog. She reached down and petted it, then straightened, finger combed her hair and walked up the brick path to the house.

She knocked on the door once.

Inside she heard squealing and laughter, which made her even more apprehensive. It sounded as if the kids were back in fine form. Then the squealing came closer and the door opened revealing Brody, hair mussed, laughing, Chrissy on his hip and Corey clinging to his leg, tugging on the tails of a shirt that had come free of Brody's blue jeans.

"Hey, there," he said, still grinning as he stepped aside to let Hannah in. "I was just helping Mom out."

"By making the kids crazy wild," Mrs. Harcourt said, joining them in the entrance of the home.

Hannah tried to keep her attention on the twins, but was having a hard time not being distracted by the beautiful house and how it was finished. The floor of the foyer was tiled with cream-colored marble. Ahead of her was an expanse of walnut doors that, she suspected, covered closets for hanging up coats. She glanced through the etched-glass partition and caught a glimpse of walnut cabinetry, brown-speckled granite countertops and slate flooring.

Very beautiful. Very chic. Not a typical rancher home at all. What had she done, letting Mrs. Harcourt take care of her rowdy and messy kids?

But then the older woman came into the foyer. She was barefoot, wearing faded old jeans and no makeup, her hair pulled back in a loose ponytail, and looking as casual as she had when she first picked the children up. Hannah relaxed.

"Mama," Chrissy said, leaning toward her, her lips stained red and a smear of what looked like yogurt on her cheeks.

"Just wait, honey," Brody's mom said, pulling a cloth out of her pocket and giving Chrissy's cheeks a quick swipe. "Sorry about that," she said to Hannah as Chrissy fought Mrs. Harcourt, then reached for Hannah again. "I was feeding them a snack when Brody came in and started roughhousing."

"Sure. Blame it on me," Brody said, bending over to pick up Corey, who was still clinging to his leg. "Dad was the one who was making them goofy."

Mr. Harcourt made an appearance behind his wife, resting his hands on her shoulders, smiling at Hannah. Winston Harcourt had brown eyes and silver hair the same shade as his beard and mustache, giving him a kindly, friendly look. He wore blue jeans and a denim shirt that had the worn and faded look of a favorite item of clothing. "Welcome to our humble home," he said. "And in my defense, I was just trying to get Corey to eat his yogurt."

"Corey never eats yogurt," Hannah said in surprise.

"Apparently he does if you make horse noises," Mrs. Harcourt said, laughing.

"Not something I'm very good at, I'm afraid," Hannah returned.

"It's my specialty," Mr. Harcourt said, pretending to snap nonexistent suspenders. "I was going to take my act on the road, but there wasn't much money in it."

Hannah chuckled at that and then heard a timer go off in the kitchen. Her cue to go.

"Thank you so much for taking care of the children. Let me know how much I owe you," she said.

She heard a dramatic gasp from Brody and looked over in time to see him holding one hand on his chest as he dragged in a noisy breath, his other hand stretched out as if seeking support.

"Are you okay?" she asked, feeling a beat of concern.

He relaxed his pose and shot a grin at his mother, who was just shaking her head. "You just crossed a serious line," he said.

"What? How?" Hannah's concern grew full-fledged.

"You never, ever offer to pay my mother for anything," Brody said in mock horror. "She gets all squirrelly and flustered and then she gets angry. And you don't want to unleash the beast."

Mrs. Harcourt released a long-suffering sigh. "Just ignore him," she said. "There's no beast unleashing going on here. But I don't want you to pay me. I offered to take care of your children because I wanted to help you out." She gave Corey, who was now sitting on the floor tugging at his shoes, an affectionate look. "It was entirely my pleasure."

"In fact, Gina probably thinks she should pay you for taking care of your children," Winston said.

"Yeah. Like rent," Brody put in.

Hannah laughed at that, surprised how at ease she felt with people she barely knew. Surprised at how relaxed Brody was. Their house might be like a show home but they seemed like down-to-earth folk.

Mrs. Harcourt looked back at her husband. "Can you take the casserole out of the oven?"

"That's not my specialty," he said.

"I have faith in you," she said, giving him a gentle

push. Then she turned back to Hannah. "So of course you are staying for supper?"

An automatic protest sprang to Hannah's lips, but it was as if Mrs. Harcourt had seen it coming and held up her hand to stop her. "I know you're going to say no, but I also know that by the time you get back to town you'll be tired and the twins will be cranky. You won't feel like cooking."

Hannah never felt like cooking after working all day, but she wasn't about to let Brody's mother know that the twins' usual supper consisted of whatever she could convince them to eat. Usually grilled cheese sandwiches.

"I feel like I've imposed on you enough," she said, unable to keep herself from looking over at Brody, who was watching her with a peculiar look in his eyes. But as soon as their eyes connected, he blinked and it seemed to disappear.

"You can keep trying to protest," Brody said, bending over to swing Corey up in his arms, "but I know how stubborn and persuasive my mom can be. You may as well give in now and save yourself a lot of energy."

Hannah bit her lip, as if thinking, but then Chrissy stretched away from Hannah, reaching for Brody's mom. Hannah would have overbalanced and fallen if Mrs. Harcourt hadn't taken the little girl out of her arms.

"I guess Chrissy settled it," she said triumphantly. And before Hannah could lodge another objection, Mrs. Harcourt was walking back into the kitchen bobbing Chrissy in her arms.

"Like I said, don't argue with my mom," Brody said, tucking his shirt back into his pants. "She doesn't always play fair."

"She sure doesn't," Hannah said as she caught a whiff of the casserole Brody's father was taking out of the oven. Her stomach growled so loudly she was sure Brody heard. "Not with smells like that coming from the kitchen."

"You may as well stay," Brody said, his voice growing quiet. "Mom loves to help out and she would be pleased if you stayed for supper."

Hannah chanced a look at Brody, who was watching her, a half grin on his face. And for a moment she wondered if he was pleased about the idea, as well.

"Thanks for dinner, Mom," Brody said, wiping his mouth and setting his napkin on his plate. "Amazing as usual."

"Glad you could join us instead of eating cold cereal in your cabin," his mother said.

"I cook. What do you think all those pots and pans I have in my cabin are for?" Brody protested, feeling a need to defend himself and not sound so much like a bachelor.

"Just because a chicken has wings doesn't mean it can fly," his dad put in with a wry grin.

"His idea of cooking is scrambling eggs," his mother said to Hannah, as if she needed to be brought up to speed on Brody's cooking habits. "And haute cuisine is using seasoning salt instead of regular salt."

"The twins and I eat a lot of scrambled eggs, as well," Hannah said, looking over at Brody with a shy smile. "It's easy to make after a long day of work. That, and grilled cheese sandwiches."

He returned her smile, feeling a moment of culinary kinship.

She held his gaze a split second longer than necessary, then turned her attention back to her daughter. The little girl opened her mouth for the spoonful of food Hannah had scooped up, then, at the last moment, spun her head away, smearing the food all over her cheeks.

"That's no way to treat such a delicious supper." Hannah put her arm around Chrissy to hold her still and quickly swiped a napkin across her daughter's dirty cheeks before she could turn again.

"You're really good at that," Brody said, full of admiration.

"I have my specialties, too," she said with a smile. And there it was again. That jolt he always felt around her.

When his mother had offered to take care of Hannah's children, he knew he would have a hard time keeping his reaction to her in perspective. He had hoped that he could be practical about it, but seeing her in his parents' home with her children felt as if parts of a puzzle had finally come together.

It felt too right, which made him even more cautious around her. Hannah had a better man in her past and Brody wasn't keen on trying to play second fiddle.

Corey, sitting between Brody and his mother, started fussing, banging his spoon on the table. He turned to Brody and held out the noodle-encrusted spoon as if giving him a treasure, babbling his encouragement.

"Why, thanks, little guy," Brody said, carefully taking it from him and setting it on his plate. Corey then handed him the plate with food still sticking to it. Brody took that, as well. "Anything else?"

Corey looked directly at him, shook his head and clearly said, "No. Sanks."

Brody laughed out loud and ruffled the boy's curly hair with his hand. "You're a little charmer, aren't you?"

Corey held up his arms and Brody lifted him off the pillows his mother had piled onto the chair for the little boy. He was about to put him on the floor when Corey reached out and grabbed Brody by the neck.

It felt as natural as could be for Brody to put his arms around him and hold him close, and when Corey tucked his head into Brody's neck, Brody felt his heart give a little stutter.

He caught Hannah watching them, her expression tinged with sorrow. Guilt suffused him. He felt as if he had usurped David's place in Corey's life. He thought he should apologize, but then Corey pushed himself upright and squirmed away from Brody.

Chrissy shoved at her plate and also tried to get out of her chair, yelling at him as if telling him to wait for her to join him.

"I'm sorry," Hannah apologized as she tried to restrain her daughter. "Once they're done eating—"

"Don't you worry about it," Winston said, smiling at Hannah. "We always had the same problem with Brody. He could never sit still once his belly was full inside and out. Man, that kid could smear food. Made such a mess we had to put down newspapers under his chair to catch all the food. Part of the reason we got Chance. Our dog."

"Outgrew that particular trait about twenty-eight years ago, Dad," Brody cut in. "And many others, I might add." He sent his father a warning glance. The last thing he needed was embarrassing blasts from his past paraded in front of Hannah.

"Thank goodness we all grow up," his mother said.

Hannah stood, picked up Chrissy with one arm, dropped her on one hip and started stacking the plates with quick efficient moves.

"You stop right there," his mom said, whisking away the plates Hannah had already stacked up. "Winston and I will do the dishes. Brody, you can help Hannah wash up the twins."

Brody shot his mother a look, but she was busy clearing the table and didn't catch it. Didn't or wouldn't. He wasn't sure which.

"I don't need any help," Hannah protested.

"I don't mind," Brody said. He could see Hannah was about to object again, but he preempted her by simply catching Corey by the pants, pulling him back and scooping him up into his arms. "Bathroom is down the hall, first door to the right."

"Isn't it always?"

Brody released a laugh as he led the way. Her sense of humor surprised him every time it popped out.

He pulled open the linen closet in the bathroom and set out a couple of hand towels and facecloths on the countertop.

But Hannah wasn't paying attention. Instead, she was turning around, her eyes wide with amazement. "This room is close to the size of my apartment."

"I think it's a reaction to the tiny house my parents lived in on the ranch in Texas," Brody said, setting Corey down on the counter beside one of the sinks. "When we bought this place and moved into the small log cabin, my dad promised my mother that he would build her the house he always felt she deserved. He took the Texas mentality and transferred it to our Montana ranch."

"You lived in Texas? I wouldn't have guessed."

Brody shrugged as he turned on the tap. "My mother came from Canada originally, and she wouldn't let a single y'all come out of our mouths."

Hannah's laughter made him feel slightly humorous. "Does she let you say 'eh'?"

"Now you're just stereotyping," he said. "But Dad and Mom, they're two different buckets of possums."

"I'm guessing that's a Texas saying."

"You want Texas talk, get my dad going. He's a live dictionary. Can speak ten words a second with gusts up to fifty."

Hannah's laughter burst out of her, and it made Brody smile just to hear it. Even Chrissy, who had been fussing up to then, started giggling.

"Your parents are very nice," she said as she wet a facecloth and wiped Chrissy's mouth. "It means a lot that they helped me out."

"My mom was pretty stoked to be able to take care of your kids," Brody said, wetting a facecloth himself. "I'm glad you let her."

"I didn't have a lot of choice, and, not going to lie, I was a bit apprehensive. But this worked out well." She looked over at him and once again it was as if he couldn't look away. "By the way, I got a call from Lilibeth Shoemaker. She said she's able to meet with us tomorrow at the café in the afternoon. Does that work for you?"

"Lunch should work." It would make things tight for him. He and his father were talking about moving cows over the next few days, but if it meant having lunch with Hannah again, he figured they could put it off a week or more.

"That's good. I'd like to report back to Mayor Shaw as soon as possible." Her brown eyes held his a moment longer than necessary.

She was just being friendly, he reminded himself, but even as the practical corner of his brain told him that, the other didn't want to deny the reality that each time they were together, something undefinable was happening between them. But did he dare let it go anywhere?

Chapter Six

Brody stepped into the café, blinking as his eyes transitioned from the bright sun outside to the inside of Great Gulch Grub.

"If you're looking for Hannah, she's in the back," Mert said with a smirk as she dropped a stack of menus in the holder at the end of the checkout counter. "Your usual spot."

"Thanks, Mert," he said, giving her a warning look.

She gave him a sly wink. "Don't need to look all scowly. Your secret is safe with me."

"What secret?" Brody asked, choosing to play dumb.

"Oh, c'mon. You've liked that girl for years. I've been watching you, and I think she's ready to have someone in her life."

Brody wanted to brush off her comment, but the part of him that had always been attracted to Hannah clung to Mert's assurance.

"You're a good man, Brody Harcourt," Mert said, looking serious. "I think she could do worse."

"Thanks. I think."

Mert just laughed and Brody made his way to the back of the café, returning the greetings he got from some of the patrons, suddenly wondering if more people knew what Mert did. Wondering, as he approached Hannah, if she did.

"Hey, there," he said as he slipped into the booth across from her, dropping his hat on the seat beside him.

Hannah looked up, and her broad smile ignited a glimmer of expectation.

"So, we'll try this again," she said.

Brody didn't mind if Lilibeth didn't show up again. It would mean spending more time with Hannah one-on-one.

Mert came by and filled their cups with coffee and asked if they needed anything. Brody shook his head, and Mert left.

He was about to say something to Hannah, when he saw Lilibeth flounce into the café wearing tight blue jeans with a loose denim shirt that revealed a pink T-shirt underneath, clinging to her curves. And when she saw Brody and Hannah, her lips parted in a generous smile. Brody sighed as she sauntered toward them. She was the reason he and Hannah were meeting here, but he had hoped to have a few more moments alone with Hannah.

"Hey, there," Lilibeth said, standing by the booth, twirling a strand of blond hair around a long-nailed finger. "You said you wanted to talk to me?"

Brody stood and gave her a polite smile as she slipped into the booth. Then he grabbed a chair from a nearby table and set it at the open end of the booth. As he dropped into it, he caught Lilibeth's disappointed pout and he congratulated himself on escaping an awkward situation.

"Are those about the contest?" Lilibeth asked, pointing a taloned finger at the papers Hannah held. She waved Mert off when she came around with the coffeepot again.

"They are. And we found out why Alanna won," Hannah said quietly, glancing from Lilibeth to the papers after Mert left. "She had a strong horsemanship mark."

Lilibeth tapped her finger on the table and sighed. "That's rotten. I thought I did pretty good with Rowdy."

"At any other time you might have won," Hannah assured her, her voice soft and well modulated. "But Alanna was especially adept at handling her horse, and the fact that she did so much groundwork—"

"Those were just tricks," Lilibeth protested. "Making her horse bow and dance along with her."

"But they made the judges take notice," Hannah said. "I'm sorry you didn't win, though. You do seem upset about it."

"I am. I tried so hard. I just wanted…wanted to be like my sisters. They always won. I just wanted them to pay attention to me for a change."

Her comment was the perfect opportunity for Brody to jump in, and without thinking he placed his hand on Hannah's to stop her from saying anything. "Is it just your sisters' attention you want? Or was it also the community's?"

"Of course I wanted the people in Jasper Gulch to notice me. It's always been about my sisters, and this time I wanted it to be about me."

"So, if you want attention, would you do other things besides entering the Miss Jasper Gulch contest to get it?" he pressed.

"What do you mean?"

Brody sent up a quick prayer. This was where things could get awkward. He wished he didn't have to do this, but he and Hannah had been asked to look into the theft. And if Lilibeth was, in fact, the L.S. of the mysterious note Cord had received, they had to follow through.

"Do you know anything about the time capsule theft?" Brody asked, deciding to simply go for broke.

Lilibeth dropped back in the booth, her arms crossed tightly, her features shifting. "Why would I?"

Her evasive answer raised suspicion. "But do you?" Brody continued, not allowing himself to be moved into a defensive position.

Lilibeth's features grew tight. "Do you think I stole the time capsule?"

"We don't know who stole it. The committee looking into this theft received a note that said if we wanted to know more about the theft we should be looking at someone with the initials L.S. Which, unfortunately, are the same as yours." Brody stopped there, hoping Lilibeth would jump to the conclusion herself without his having to make an accusation.

"Is that what you're thinking? That I stole that time capsule? Why would I? I was as excited as everyone else to see what was in it." Then, to Brody's surprise, he saw the sparkle of tears in her eyes. "I know I'm not the smartest or the prettiest or the best…horse person. But I'm not a thief. I love my town and I love the people in it." Her voice broke and Brody felt like the lowest heel. He patted her awkwardly on the hand while Hannah handed her a tissue. Lilibeth wiped her eyes, blew her nose and looked from Hannah to Brody. "Do other people believe I did that? That I would do something like that?"

Brody bit his lip, wishing, once again, he didn't have to do this. "It was because of the anonymous note that we felt we needed to talk to you. That's all."

"Anonymous. Of course it was. It was probably that lousy Pete Daniels who wrote it. Little weasel. He tried to ask me out once but I turned him down. And I heard him whining the other day about how people don't appreciate how hard he's had it." Lilibeth's eyes grew hard. "He's probably just trying to pin this on me to get even."

Brody felt a flash of sympathy for her. "We will talk to him about this for sure, but we were just following the lead of the note. I'm so sorry we thought you might be a suspect. But we want to get the bottom of what happened to the capsule. Especially with all the other centennial celebrations going on."

"Like the basket auction," Lilibeth said, looking at Hannah.

She nodded. "Yes."

"That does it. I'm entering that auction," she said, slapping her palm on the table. "So now, I gotta go. I got work to do." She slid out of the booth and without another glance at either Brody or Hannah, she strode out of the café, a girl on a mission.

As the door closed behind her, Brody blew out a sigh and shoved his hand through his hair. "That was tough," he said. "I still feel bad that we had to do it." He put the chair back by the table and as he sat down, Mert came by with refills for their coffee.

Hannah put her hand over her cup. "No, thanks, Mert. I should get back to work."

Brody tamped down his disappointment. He had hoped to share another cup of coffee with her. Some coffee and some more time.

But he stood and pulled out his wallet, dropping a few bills on the table the same time as Hannah drew her own wallet out of her purse.

"This is on me," he said.

"Thank you." She put her wallet back.

He dropped his hat on his head and stood aside as she slipped the folder inside her purse and slung it over her shoulder. Then he followed her out of the café. A breeze had sprung up, sending errant papers scurrying down the street and stealing the warmth of the afternoon sun.

Outside, she stopped and turned to him.

"I just want to say that you managed the meeting with Lilibeth very diplomatically," Hannah said, giving him a gentle smile.

"Diplomacy isn't usually my strong point," he said with a half grin. "I've been accused many times of being too quick to speak my mind."

"I wouldn't say that. You were remarkably restrained when Mayor Shaw made that comment to you." She was looking down at the papers as she spoke, running her fingernail along the edges. "I…I'm sorry he felt like he needed to warn you that way. I didn't think it was necessary."

Brody wanted to shrug off her comment, but something in the way she said it raised a question about why she felt the need to assure him. "I haven't heard the nickname Book-it Brody for a while."

"Was it deserved?"

"At one time, yes." His smile faded as he held her eyes. For a moment he felt a sense of affinity with Lilibeth. He wanted Hannah to know the truth about him, not what people were saying. "But I don't think people can accuse me of tearing wildly around the countryside anymore. I've settled down since then. I'm not the risk-taker I used to be."

Hannah gave him an enigmatic look. "But your job—"

"It's not as risky as people think. Sure, there are

times when hard decisions need to be made, but I have
backup. I have my team and my training. And it's a job
that needs to be done." A job that he was proud of doing.
When the opportunity came up for him to become a
firefighter, he'd jumped at it. He wanted to serve the
community. To show that he was someone who could
be depended on.

"A man of honor," she said quietly, her words creating a curious feeling of pride that he hadn't felt in a
while.

"Thanks for that," he said.

She waited a moment, as if she wanted to say something more, then gave him a quick smile, clutched her
purse close to her and stepped out into the street.

Just as a truck sped around the corner, tires squealing.

Brody didn't think, he simply acted. He hooked his
arm around Hannah and pulled her back just as the
truck blew past them, tires squealing. Brody caught a
quick glimpse of the driver who hadn't even turned to
see what he had done.

Pete Daniels.

He would have a word with that weasel, as Lilibeth
called him. But first he had to see to Hannah, who
sagged against him.

"Are you okay?" he asked, turning her to face him.

Her one hand clung to his waist, the other his shoulder. Her face was pale, her eyes bright.

"Yeah. I'm okay. A little shook up." She shifted, as if
trying to get her balance, but Brody didn't let go of her
and she didn't look as if she wanted to leave.

A breeze picked up a strand of hair, dropping it
across her face. It clung to her lips and Brody gave in

to an impulse and brushed it away, his hand lingering, then coming to rest on her shoulder.

They stood this way a moment, standing close, eyes locked.

He wanted to kiss her.

His heart skipped a beat as his breath slowed. Then she stepped back from him and the moment was blown away with the wind swirling down the street. A passing truck honked at them and Brody waved absently, not even bothering to see whether it was for him or Hannah.

Then he wondered if anyone had seen them and what people would think. Book-it Brody and David's widow.

"Thanks for the coffee," she said, hitching her purse up on her shoulder. Then, without another word, she glanced up and down the street and hurried across.

Brody puffed up his cheeks and blew out a breath, feeling a bit shook up at his reaction to holding Hannah.

And how right it felt.

"If there's anything else you need, let me know." Hannah came around her desk and handed a folder of papers she had just photocopied to Robin Frazier, who was waiting in the foyer of the town hall. "Sorry it took so long to get them together for you. Olivia picked up some of the minutes of old town meetings. I know you two have been working together, she might have something if you can't find it in here."

"Please. Don't worry about it," Robin said, waving off her apology. "I know you're busy with the fair and the basket auction. Someday I want to know more about the history of that."

Hannah couldn't help her quick glance at the large clock hanging on the wall behind Robin, one of the few artifacts remaining from the building's history as a bank. The minute hand was ticking onto five o'clock. The ranch was a twenty-five-minute drive. She was already later than usual.

"But not today," Robin hastily amended, tucking the folder into a large leather messenger bag that she slung over her neck, then slipping her blond hair free from the strap. "I know you want to leave to pick up your children."

"Yes. My mother usually takes care of the twins, but she's been ill."

"I heard about your mother. How is she?"

"I talked to my father this afternoon. She's been running a fever, but the doctor said they just had to wait for the antibiotics to kick in." Hannah had to fight down a surge of worry. Her parents were such a support to her, it was hard to see her mother sick. "Gina Harcourt is babysitting for me and I don't want to take advantage of her generosity." She knew this was only part of the reason for her rush. Deep down, she knew it had as much to do with Brody and that moment they had shared this afternoon on the street outside the café.

The entire afternoon her thoughts had slipped back to that moment and how it had felt to be held by him. Protected.

Sure, she was an independent woman. She had to be, raising two kids on her own, but there were times when the loneliness bit at her. Times when she wished she had someone who had her back.

"You're so lucky to have family around to help you out."

The wistful note in Robin's voice made Hannah want to ask her more, but then the door to the foyer opened again and Hannah fought a sigh. Abigail Rose came marching toward her desk, her hand clutching a paper and her eyes focused like a laser on Hannah, her permed hair bobbing with each step. She looked like a woman on a mission and Hannah prayed that mission wasn't her or her twins, though she couldn't think why. The twins were out of the apartment all day. Last night, after coming back from the ranch, they went to sleep without a peep. Surely they couldn't have bothered her.

"Have you and Brody had a chance to meet with Lilibeth Shoemaker?" she demanded.

Relief sluiced through Hannah. Thankfully, she and her twins were off the hook. "Yes. We did," she said.

"Find anything out?"

Hannah wasn't about to give her a report in front of Robin. "Whatever we have to say I'll bring to the attention of the committee."

"Maybe we should have a meeting tomorrow," Abigail said.

Hannah thought of all the work she had to do yet. The clock in the foyer wasn't the only one ticking. The fair was set to go in a week and she was falling behind. "I don't know if it's necessary."

"Just a quick one. So we know what's up before the fair starts."

"As long as it is a very short meeting at the end of the day." That way, if anyone got long-winded, she could cite having to pick up her children as her excuse to leave.

"We can do that. And now I need to talk to Mayor Shaw," Abigail announced.

"He's not in right now," Hannah said. "Did you want to leave a message for him?"

"Yes. He needs to know I've been talking around. A bunch of townspeople want to get a petition going to get the proceeds from this picnic basket auction to go to the museum." Abigail turned to Robin and pointed a finger at her. "You. You're working with Olivia on that museum. I'm right, aren't I? About the museum needing the money. It doesn't need to go to that bridge, that's for sure."

Robin raised one hand in a gesture of surrender. "Sorry I can't help you. I don't have any input into what money from which fund-raiser goes where. I'm just working with Olivia to collect information for my genealogy thesis."

"Find anything interesting?" Abigail asked in a voice that brooked no opposition to her request.

"Actually, I did. When I was at the newspaper office, I found clippings from some old papers." Robin turned to Hannah. "Did you know that Lucy Shaw, who died when her car drove off the Jasper Gulch Bridge, was engaged at the time? That must have been so hard for her fiancé."

Abigail's sudden intake of breath startled Hannah. As did the woman's suddenly laying her hand on Hannah's arm and tut-tutting in a motherly fashion. "My dear, I'm so sorry," she said, then Abigail turned to Robin. "Did you know that Hannah's husband, David, died not that long ago?" Abigail said.

"Oh, no. Hannah. I'm so sorry for being so insensitive." Robin looked genuinely distressed, and Hannah felt bad for her.

"Passing on information is not being insensitive," Hannah assured her. "Besides, David died almost two years ago now."

As she spoke the words, they took on a new reality. Two years she had been on her own. In some ways, it felt like an eternity ago, as if she was a different person then than she was now.

"Anyhow, I'm sorry for your loss," Robin continued.

"It's okay." And even as Hannah gave her assurance, she felt a measure of guilt. Was it right to feel as if she was moving on?

She shook off the question and glanced at the clock again. Right now she had her babies to think of. "I'm sorry, Robin and Abigail, but I need to lock up for the day."

A few minutes later she was in her car and on her way, letting her thoughts wander as she drove through the rolling countryside toward the Harcourt ranch. She didn't often get to take her car out of town and today she was determined to simply enjoy the ride. Yesterday she had felt rushed and tense, but today she was more relaxed.

Her thoughts wandered over the day, from her recent conversation with Robin, back to that moment she and Brody had shared as they stood together on the street. She could still feel his hands feathering her cheek as he brushed her hair away. For a frightening moment, she had thought he was going to kiss her.

And for an equally frightening moment, she had wondered what it would feel like.

Then her eyes fell on a flash of metal hanging from her rearview mirror, winking in the sun.

David's dog tags. For the first couple of months after he'd died, she had worn them around her neck as penance for how angry she was over his death. How angry she was at him for pushing her to marry him when she was entertaining doubts about their relationship.

His death had left her a widow and single mother.

She shook off the thoughts. She had gone over them so often, they were well-tilled ground. She needed to move on.

Dear Lord, she prayed as she drove. *I don't know what's happening. Don't know what I'm allowed to think. But I'm confused right now. I have my babies and my responsibilities. I don't know what I'm allowed to feel. Help me to trust in You. To trust in Your perfect love. To know that all I need is You.*

And as she drove the rest of the way to the ranch, she felt a gentle peace settle on her heart as she laid her concerns in God's hands.

"Dear Hannah, we are at the corrals with the kids. Just go past the log house and around the barn."

Hannah read the note taped to the door of Mrs. Harcourt's house, then headed toward the corrals. The sun was warm on the top of her head and she pulled her sweater off and tied it around her waist, enjoying the outside air and the open spaces of the ranch, sending up a prayer of thanks that Gina Harcourt had offered to take in her children.

Every day, when she came back to the stuffy apartment, she always felt sorry for her children stuck inside day after day. Though she was thankful for her mother's help, she knew she couldn't expect her to take the children out regularly. As well, after a long day of work, Hannah didn't have the energy herself to take them out for a walk. The twins were always hungry and cranky by the time she was done with work. So it was often a quick supper, bath, a story and then bed. Saturdays, she would take them to the park to make up for their having to spend every day cooped up, but every time she did, she wished they could experience this more often.

Now they were being taken care of on a ranch, with wide-open spaces, and every day they were taken out into the fresh afternoon air.

She came closer to the log house the note mentioned and her steps slowed. A black pickup truck was parked in front of it. She guessed it was Brody's from the decal on the back window that showed the logo of the Jasper Gulch Firefighters and below it their motto, Fighting What You Fear.

She heard Brody's deep quiet voice coming from behind the barn and her heart quickened in anticipation.

She walked around the barn and the first thing she saw was Brody, mounted on a horse, walking away from her. His head was bent over as he talked. Winston walked alongside, his hands in his pockets, his uneven gait and bowed legs a testimony to many years in the saddle. She couldn't quell her anxiety when she saw the horse. Though she knew it was silly, she just plain didn't like horses. They gave her the willies.

Then she heard Corey's giggle just as Brody turned the horse and she saw her son sitting in front of Brody on the saddle.

Her heart plunged at the sight of her little boy sitting so far off the ground. He was so small. So vulnerable. What if he fell? It was such a long way down and those hooves of those horses—she knew firsthand exactly how hard they could be.

"Hello, Hannah."

Hannah spun around at the sound of Mrs. Harcourt's voice, her heart still pounding with reaction.

Brody's mom walked toward her, holding Chrissy, grinning. "Your little guy sure likes riding the horse."

"Can Brody please take him off that thing, Mrs. Harcourt?" she asked, reaching out a hand as if pleading.

"Please call me Gina… Are you okay?" the woman asked with concern. "You look a little pale."

"I don't like to see my boy on a horse. They give me the creeps."

"Horses?"

It wasn't too hard to hear Gina's incredulous tone, but Hannah couldn't stop the fear building in her voice. "I…I got bucked off one when I was a teenager." Though it had been years ago, watching her little guy on that animal could still re-create the panicky feeling of helplessness she had experienced. She had slipped off the saddle and caught her foot in the stirrup and the horse went crazy.

She still had a scar on the back of her head and one on her shoulder to show for her misadventure. She had been with Adam Shaw when it happened. He had pleaded with her not to tell anyone. And neither of them had, though, later on, she had told Julie. Her friend had tried a number of times to convince her that horses were fine. But Hannah had never sat on the back of a horse since.

"Please, take him down," she asked again.

Brody came near with Corey, his head still bent over as he laughed at Corey's antics.

"Hannah isn't comfortable with Corey on the horse," Gina called out to her son. "Could you take him off?"

Hannah clung to the top rail of the fence, the rough wood digging into her palm as she watched, trying to stifle her irrational worry, but all she could think of was her little boy falling to the dirt and being kicked by those large hooves.

Brody pushed his hat back on his head as if to see her better and Hannah saw his frown as he held Corey closer, but she didn't care. She wanted her son back on the ground. In her arms. "He likes it."

"Please," Hannah begged.

"Oh, honey, this isn't Brody's first rodeo," Winston assured her. "Boy was practically born on a horse."

But Hannah kept her gaze on Corey, unable to keep the pleading look off her face. Brody looked down at Corey again and then, without another word, slowly dismounted, holding her son close while he did. He looped the reins over the horse's head, leaving them to dangle in the dirt. Then he slowly walked over to Hannah and handed him her son.

Hannah grabbed Corey, clinging to him as her heart slowed. "Thanks" was all she could say.

"Are you okay?"

"I am now."

"Hannah told me she was bucked off a horse when she was younger," Gina said, coming to join her with Chrissy. "That's why she's afraid."

Brody looked taken aback. As if he couldn't comprehend this emotion. "But you like the rodeo."

"As long as someone else is riding and the horses are in an arena, I'm okay." Though when she'd watched Ryan, Julie's now-fiancé, riding saddle broncs at the rodeo, it had been hard not to get nervous.

"I wouldn't have let anything happen to him." Brody sounded hurt at her concern.

"I know. But it's just…I'm his mother and I'm the one solely responsible for him."

"That must be hard," Brody said, reaching over to brush some straw off Corey's hair. "I'm sorry I made you worry."

His understanding eased the tension out of her shoulders. "It's silly. I know. But I just feel so vulnerable when it comes to my kids."

"Of course you do," Gina said, patting her on the

shoulder. "You lost someone you love and that makes you feel helpless."

Hannah nodded, still holding Corey close. But even as her fear was eased away, another emotion was making itself known as Brody's hand rested lightly on her shoulder. She guessed it was in sympathy, but too easily it re-created the same emotions she had felt around him this afternoon. Then she looked up into his dark eyes and caught a curious light in them under the brim of his cowboy hat. Her breath slowed a moment and she felt as if she was losing herself in his eyes just as she had on Main Street. She didn't want to look away. She felt a tingle in her shoulder where his hand still rested. Warm, large and strong. Since David's death, she hadn't felt anything like this around any man.

"Mommy. Mommy," Chrissy's insistent voice called out, and Hannah felt herself snap back into reality.

What was she thinking? She had her children. David's children. They were her first responsibility.

Brody wished everything could stop here. He didn't want to move. Just wanted to stay on this spot, looking down at Hannah, his hand resting on her shoulder. Just like this afternoon she wasn't looking away, either. Did she feel it, too?

Hannah blinked, gave her head a shake as if bringing herself back to reality, then gave Brody a careful smile. "My fear of horses must seem strange to you," she said as she pressed a kiss to Corey's head. "And I'm sorry if I sounded panicky."

"No. That's fine," Brody said, dropping his hand to his side. "We should have asked. We won't do it again."

"Thank you," she said quietly, holding Corey close

to her. Then she looked down at her watch. "I should get going."

But Brody heard a curious reluctance in her voice.

"Do you have to go back right away, Hannah?" his mother was asking. "We wanted to show the twins the new kittens that Loco had. Their eyes just opened yesterday."

Hannah looked from Corey to Brody and a gentle smile curved her lips. "I love kittens. I'm sure the kids would enjoy seeing them."

"Don't let the mother cat's name fool you," Brody assured Hannah. "She's very tame."

"I should be okay. I haven't had any traumatic kitten experiences," she said, adding a grin to her comment. "A few scratches from Julie's, but I think I'm over that now."

He laughed at that. "Then let's go."

"Oh, dear," his mother said, making a show of looking at her watch. "Honey, could you take this little peanut?" she asked, handing Chrissy to him. "I completely forgot. I need to check my roast." Then she turned to Hannah. "We'd love to have you join us for supper again. If that's okay with you."

Hannah hesitated but only for a moment. "As long as the kids behave—"

"They both had a long nap. They should be okay," his mother assured her.

"Are you going to unsaddle Hardscrabble?" his father asked him as he tied the horse's reins to the fence. "I've got to go help your mother peel potatoes."

Brody wanted to ask his father why he was suddenly so domesticated but didn't want to draw attention to what was going on. He suspected his parents were playing a heavy-handed game of matchmaker.

"I'll put him away," he assured his father, hoping he got the hint to lay low.

Winston just grinned, tugged on his cowboy hat and ambled away from the corrals, whistling for Chance to follow him.

"The kittens are in the back corner of the barn," Brody said, shifting Chrissy to his hip and pulling on the large metal handle of the door. It rumbled open and though the air outside was warm, inside the barn was dark and cool. Brody flicked a switch and a watery light shone from a few lightbulbs strung up from the beams of the ceiling, shining on the center aisle flanked by wooden stalls. "It's a bit gloomy in here. Hope you can see okay," he said, shooting a glance behind her.

"This reminds me of one of the barns on the Shaw ranch," Hannah said, looking around. "We would play hide-and-seek in the loft. I always lost because Julie, Faith and Adam knew the best hiding spots."

"You and Julie are good friends, aren't you?" Brody shifted Chrissy on his hip as he walked down the main aisle of the barn, his feet echoing in the quiet.

"Best friends. I don't know how I would have gotten through that time after David's death without her."

"That must have been difficult for you." Brody didn't want to talk about David, but he had been a part of Hannah's life and he was the father of her kids.

"It was." She released a light laugh. "But everything happened so quickly. David graduated basic training, we got married, he shipped out and next thing I know, I'm a widow and expecting twins."

Her comment created an awkward silence and Brody wondered how much she missed David. They had been together since grade school, after all.

And she had a large picture of him on her desk.

So he said nothing as he turned into the farthest stall where the kittens were. Loco, a tortoiseshell cat, was curled up in a large wooden box, surrounded by five little balls of fluff. Some were tabby, some tricolor like their mother, and one was black. His mother had laid down a blanket this afternoon when she had gone to see if the kittens' eyes were open, so he set Chrissy down on it and bent over to pick up a tiny tabby kitten.

"Oh, my goodness. Aren't they adorable?" Hannah said, crouching down and setting Corey on the blanket beside his sister.

Brody knelt down beside Chrissy and gently laid the mewling kitten in her lap. The little girl waved her hands in excitement, then reached down and patted the kitten's head.

"That's right, Chrissy," Brody said, brushing a knuckle alongside the kitten's face. "Nice and gentle."

Corey squealed and leaned over, grabbing the side of the box, but Hannah pulled him back and scooped up a tiny kitten as well, holding it in her hands to show her son. "Be careful," Hannah said as she brought the kitten closer to him. He made a grab for the kitten, but Hannah snatched it back just in time. "Gentle," she admonished quietly, taking his hand and showing him what to do. Corey batted the kitten again and once again Hannah patiently demonstrated, holding his hand in hers. Finally he seemed to understand, and a few moments later Hannah placed the kitten on his lap, as well.

"They're so cute," Brody said, shifting so he was now sitting on the blanket.

"Who can't like kittens?" Hannah scooped up another one and held it close, rubbing her nose over the tiny head.

"I meant your kids are cute."

Hannah looked up at him, the kitten still cuddled up against her face, looking surprisingly childlike. Her features were relaxed and she didn't seem as tense as when he'd met her the first time. Her smile dived into his heart. "Well, you're talking to the wrong person about them. I think my kids are adorable, even when they've got chocolate pudding smeared all over their mouths."

He felt a gentle contentment easing into his soul and he wanted to touch her again. To connect with her.

Chrissy patted the kitten again and then pushed it away, lurching to her feet.

"Chrissy. Gentle," Hannah admonished her.

"The kitten is fine," Brody said, rescuing the kitten as Chrissy tottered a moment, trying to get her balance on the bunched-up blanket. "Here you go," he said to the mother cat, laying her baby beside her. Loco sniffed the kitten, as if making sure it was still hers, gave it a few licks, then looked over at the kitten Hannah still held.

"Okay, I get the message," Hannah said, also putting her and Corey's kittens back. She took a moment to stroke Loco's head as if assuring her, then picked up her son and swung him into her arms.

"He's getting kind of big for you, isn't he?" Brody said, picking Chrissy up, as well.

"It's not him as much as the two of them combined. That's why church can be so difficult."

"Did you enjoy attending on Sunday?" Brody asked as they walked out of the barn toward the house.

She gave him a shy smile and a nod. "I did. And I meant to thank you and your parents for your help. It was nice to go to church again."

"I'm glad we could help you out."

"And thanks for taking my son out on the horse. I know I sounded…irrational, but my reaction was the result of a combination of factors. Ever since the twins were born, I've felt overly protective of them."

"I'm guessing much of that has to do with David's death."

"Partly. Losing David made me realize how fragile life is, and it also, like I told your mother, made me feel more vulnerable."

"I wouldn't have done anything to hurt Corey." Brody felt he needed to assure her of that. "You can trust me."

Hannah looked over at him and then gave him a careful smile. "I know that."

Her quiet affirmation created an answering warmth and a faint hope.

Once again he held her gaze. Once again he wanted to touch her. To make a connection beyond the eye contact they seemed to be indulging in over the past few days.

But he was holding her child and they were getting closer to the house where his parents waited.

And he was sure they were watching them with overly avid interest.

"So, Brody and Hannah, tell us what you found out so we can all get back to our business." Cord stood, resting his hips against the table of the meeting room, his arms folded across his chest, clearly telegraphing his annoyance with this sudden meeting of the committee.

Hannah didn't blame him. She thought this meeting was a waste of time as well, but on the other hand, the sooner they could clear Lilibeth's name, the sooner they could look elsewhere.

"Do we have enough members present?" Abigail asked.

"We're not voting on anything," Cal reminded her. "So, what did you two discover?"

"Lilibeth didn't do it," Brody said.

"And how do you know that?" Abigail asked, resting her folded arms on the table in front of her. Today her nails were a virulent shade of orange that clashed mightily with her pink shirt. "Did she make eye contact with you? Did she cover her mouth or nose when she was talking? Those are signs of lying, you know."

Hannah stifled a smile. Sounded like someone was spending too much time on the internet.

"She was pretty upset when we asked her about it," Hannah said. "And, no, she didn't cover her mouth and yes, she did make eye contact. Besides, we can all agree she's not strong enough to have shifted that capsule."

"She could have had an accomplice. Been the one giving directions," Abigail insisted.

"No. She was adamant that she had no part in the theft of the time capsule," Brody said, the tapping of his booted foot on the floor telegraphing his own frustration with Abigail's comments. "And I believe her. I think she's innocent."

"Okay, then," Cal said. "We'll have to look in other directions."

"So what do we do about the note that Cord got?" Rusty drawled, leaning back in his chair.

"It could just be a prank, like we initially thought," Cord said, dragging his hand over his face.

"Lilibeth thought the note might have come from Pete Daniels," Brody said.

"Why Pete?" Cord shot him a frown.

"She mentioned that he had asked her out and she had turned him down," Hannah said. "Lilibeth thought it might have been a prank on his part. To get even."

"He does seem to be carrying a chip on his shoulder, but I can't see him involved in all of this. For now, let's just let it rest. Maybe something will come up at the fair. So, if that's all we need to discuss…" He let the sentence hang a moment. Then, when no one said anything, he pushed himself away from the table. "Okay. We'll meet in a couple of weeks, once the dust of the fair has settled."

"But we'll be going directly into the Old Tyme wedding preparations," Abigail said.

"Don't remind me," Cord groaned. "Fifty brides and fifty grooms is one hundred brides and grooms too many."

"You really don't have a romantic bone in your body, do you?" Brody joked.

"I'll save the romance for you, Harcourt," Cord snapped. "I'm just arranging the wedding for the town's celebrations. That's all."

Hannah stifled a smile at Cord's abrupt tone. She was still surprised he had allowed himself to be roped into the job.

"So, if there's nothing else, I guess we can go," Cal said, glancing at his watch.

It was now five o'clock and Hannah was anxious to get to the ranch to pick up her children.

Cord was the first one out of the room and Cal was right on his heels. Rusty and Abigail lingered, chatting as Hannah and Brody left, as well.

"Are you done at the office?" Brody asked as he and Hannah made their way down the stairs to the entrance of the town hall.

"I cleared my desk just before the meeting," Hannah said. "I'm headed to the ranch next to get the kids. I just feel bad that it went later than I hoped."

"You don't need to worry about that. You could probably stay for supper again."

Her first instinct was to say no. She felt as if she was taking advantage of Brody's mother. But the thought of going back to an empty apartment and trying to feed the kids dinner held little appeal compared to having dinner she didn't have to prepare with a family. And Brody.

"My mother is counting on it," he said as he held the door open for her. "I think she's making Chrissy's favorite."

"She already knows Chrissy has a favorite?" she said with a chuckle. "She's only been there a few times."

"Apparently, it's broccoli-stuffed chicken breasts with mashed potatoes, fresh corn from the garden and spinach salad."

"My daughter has excellent taste."

"And Corey loves chocolate pie for dessert."

"He takes after me then. It's one of my favorites, too."

"I think my mom has been doing some extracurricular research. See you back at the ranch." Brody dropped his hat back on his head and sauntered away. Hannah watched him leave, a beat of expectation rising in her chest. She stifled her perennial second thoughts and walked to her car. Moments later she was headed out of town, the lowering sun creating alluring shadows from the rolling hills. What would it be like to live out here? she wondered, mentally comparing her small, cramped apartment to the wide-open spaces she was driving through. To have a garden. To have extra room. A place for her children to play.

The very thing she was working so hard to provide for them.

She let her thoughts wander for the tiniest moment

to Brody and to the ranch she was driving toward. The mental picture was foggy and she didn't know if she dared let it solidify. But what would it be like—

A thunk in the rear of her car pulled her back into the present. She slowed, listening, but then nothing. Must have been her imagination. But she kept her speed down after that, paying attention to every sound. As a result, she was at the ranch a little later than she had hoped.

She pulled up to the Harcourt home, and before she got out of her car, Brody was out the door and striding down the sidewalk toward her in his stocking feet.

"Where were you? What happened?" He sounded upset.

"Are the kids okay?" Her heart did a flip and she was about to rush past him, when he stopped her.

"Yeah. They're fine. But you should have been here twenty minutes ago. I left town just before you did. I tried calling you on your cell phone to see what was taking so long, but you didn't answer."

The agitation in his expression was genuine, as was the concern in his voice. But she couldn't resist a little joke.

"Well, it's no surprise that I came later," she said with a half grin. "How was I supposed to keep up to Book-it Brody?"

His frown deepened and for a moment she thought he didn't appreciate her stab at humor. Then a smile teased his lips. "I wasn't driving that fast. Did you take a detour?"

"No. I don't know any detours here. I just heard a funny clunk in my car, so I took it slow. As for my cell phone, I think I shut if off during the meeting and forgot to turn it on again."

His frown returned. "We'd better take a look at your

car before you go," he said as they walked back to the house together.

"I'm sure it's nothing. The car worked just fine." She looked down at his feet. "Why aren't you wearing your boots?"

"I always take them off in Mom's house. She's obsessive about her new floors."

She chuckled at the sight of him walking over the sidewalk in his stocking feet. "And her sidewalk apparently."

"I was worried about you," he said.

She looked at him, surprised at the warmth those few words created in her. "Really?"

"Yeah. Really." His voice was quiet and they stood facing each other and, as had happened a number of times in the past few days, she felt herself getting lost in the deep brown of his eyes.

His hand touched her shoulder and she gave in to an impulse and covered it with her own. His hand tightened. Hers did, too. Their silent communication said that things were shifting between them. Changing.

Could she do this? Did she dare?

She swallowed and gave him a tremulous smile. "You were probably more worried that you'd be stuck with my kids."

"That might be what it was," he agreed, a half smile curving his lips. "But I think we both know that's not true."

She let the sentence lie between them ripe with possibilities.

Then the door opened, and Brody and Hannah both lowered their hands with record speed.

"There you are," Gina said to Hannah, sounding as relieved as Brody had sounded worried. She glanced from Hannah to Brody, her expression expectant, and Hannah wondered if her cheeks looked as flushed as they felt. Thankfully, Gina said nothing as she waved them inside. "Well, come on in, you two. Supper is ready and the twins are hungry."

"Let's not keep Their Majesties waiting," Brody said, standing aside to let Hannah precede him.

The table was already laid out, Chrissy and Corey sitting in booster seats strapped to the dining room chairs. "Look at you two, all ready to eat at the big people's table," Hannah said, bending over to brush a kiss over each of their foreheads. They were all clean and shining in their sleepers, and their hair was soft and silky and smelling of baby soap.

"I got the seats last night," Gina said. "After you left. I figured it would be easier to feed them this way than to juggle them on our laps all the time."

"You didn't have to do that," Hannah said. "I could have given you mine."

"And taken away all of Gina's fun," Winston said, coming into the dining room. "She's been stocking up on all kinds of stuff for those kidlets."

"Winston, you don't need to tell her that," Gina said, looking as if she was blushing.

"You should see all the toys and paraphernalia she's gathered together," Winston continued.

"Winston," Gina said again, her voice holding a note of reprimand.

Brody raised his eyebrows and rubbed his hands together. "Why don't we eat," he said.

Hannah sensed some awkwardness but decided it was best to do as Brody did and carry on.

"You sit down, Hannah, my dear," Gina said. "I'll get supper on the table."

"Do you need any help?" Hannah asked.

"No. Winston can give me a hand."

Brody pulled out her chair between Chrissy and Corey. "May as well sit down," he said. "The sooner we all get settled, the sooner we all can eat."

His courtly gesture created a dull ache. David used to do that, she thought as she slipped into the chair. She caught herself, wondering if she would always be using David as a yardstick in one form or another.

Then she looked over at Brody as he settled down on the other side of Corey and thoughts of David faded away.

Chapter Seven

"Tell your mom thanks again for supper," Hannah said as she clipped the buckle of Corey's car seat tight. "It was absolutely delicious."

"I'll let her know again," Brody said, setting Chrissy in her car seat on the other side of Hannah's car.

"I'm sure she called your mother to get some ideas."

"She did?" Hannah's surprise made him wonder if he should have told her. He knew his mother was campaigning heavily and he hoped Hannah didn't notice.

"My mom lives to please," he said, pulling the belt around Chrissy's arms.

"Do you need a hand?" Hannah asked as Brody tried to get Chrissy to sit still long enough so he could buckle her in.

"I'm good." He made another attempt to attach the clip but he couldn't make it reach.

Hannah came over to his side of the car and watched his struggles. Finally he had to admit defeat and step back. "I can't figure that thing out," he said.

Hannah leaned in and with a few deft moves had the straps clipped down and Chrissy was secure.

"Don't smirk," Brody warned as Hannah straightened.

"I'll try not to," she said, but her lips flirted with a grin.

Brody glanced at the waning light. "You'd better get going. Make sure you watch out for wildlife on your way home, especially moose and elk. Their eyes will shine back at you but they're so tall, you won't see them in your little car." He didn't want to imagine what a large animal like that could do to her little car and the precious cargo it held.

He and his father had checked the car but couldn't find anything wrong. Brody had tried to convince Hannah to let him drive her back but she refused. So he let it go.

"I'll drive carefully."

"And don't forget to turn your cell phone on," he warned.

"You sound like my mother."

"Is that good or bad?"

She held his eyes, her expression softening. "It's nice" was all she said. Then she turned away and slipped behind the wheel. She closed the door, started the engine, reversed out of the lot and with a wink of her taillights was headed down the road.

He watched her leave and, as he had the last time she'd driven away with the twins, he sent up a prayer for their safety.

He glanced at his parents' house. He should go and help clean up but right now he didn't want to see his mother's hopeful face and feel the pressure of her expectations. He had enough of his own, thank you very much.

So he headed back to his own house, turned on the television for noise and company and started folding the laundry he had done yesterday and had dumped on his sofa. Canned laughter filled the quiet of the house but it annoyed him. As soon as he had his clothes put away he shut off the television, dropped into the old worn recliner he'd inherited from his father and picked up the book he'd been reading. An adventure story that Dylan had recommended, but he couldn't get into it.

Visions of Hannah drifted through his head. He didn't know what to do about his attraction to her. At times it seemed she felt the same. Other times he sensed her pulling back. Was she thinking of David during those times?

Brody set the book aside with a sigh of frustration and was about to get up and go outside when his cell phone rang. He pulled it out of his pocket, grateful for the distraction.

Hannah's name showed up on the screen.

He hit the answer button. "Hello?"

"Brody…" Her voice faded away and he could hear crying in the background.

"Hannah? What's wrong? Are you okay?" The staccato questions burst out of him as he jumped to his feet, already headed to the door.

"I'm okay. The kids…the kids…they're fine." She stopped, her voice strained. "But my car is in the ditch."

"Hannah, sweetie, what happened?" Brody grabbed his keys off the hanger by the door, snatched his jacket off the table where he had left it and was out the door, running to his truck.

"I was driving and I saw something big and dark on the road. I thought it was a moose." She stopped again, as if she was trying not to cry. "I tried to avoid it, then I heard that clunk again and my car ended up going off the road."

Brody got into the truck and started it. He slammed

it into gear and spun the wheel one-handed as he reversed out of the yard. "Where are you?"

"Just on the highway. About fifteen minutes from town. I tried to call my dad..." Her voice broke again.

"You're sure you're okay? Should I call the ambulance?"

"No. I just drove into the ditch. I didn't hit anything, but I can't drive out. The car won't go ahead or back. It just runs."

"I'll be there as soon as I can." He heard her shushing one of the twins and he gunned it, flicking his own lights on high beam.

"Thanks so much."

"It'll be okay," he assured her. "Do you want me to stay on the phone?"

"No. I should see to the twins. I'll just wait here."

The setting sun cast a golden glow in the darkening sky. Brody dropped his phone in his pocket and peered through the dusk, on the lookout for wildlife. He wouldn't be any good to Hannah if he plowed into an elk or moose on his way to rescue her.

Ten minutes later he saw a set of taillights in the ditch and headlights shining toward him. He assumed the taillights were from Hannah's car. The others, probably from someone heading out of town. Brody put his lights on dim and pulled up beside Hannah's car. An older man wearing baggy overalls, a worn suit coat and a battered felt bowler hat stood beside Hannah, holding Corey. It was Alfie Hart and he looked as if he would have preferred to be anywhere but here. Hannah was rocking Chrissy, her cries piercing the night air.

Alfie saw Brody and scurried over. "Here. Take this," he said, shoving Corey into Brody's arms as if the child was a sack of feed he badly wanted to get rid of. Brody checked Corey over, but aside from the track of tears still shining on his cheeks, he looked okay.

"You going to take care of everything?" Alfie asked, edging away from them both. "I gotta get to my buddy's place. Promised him I'd help him out."

As Brody nodded, Alfie scooted off to his car, his relief evident. At least he had stopped, Brody told himself as he walked over to Hannah.

She held Chrissy close to her, shushing her as she rocked the crying baby.

"Are you okay?" he asked, putting his hand on her shoulder, squeezing lightly to assure her.

Hannah sniffed and nodded. "Just shook up. I wasn't going that fast when I hit the ditch." Her voice wavered, broke.

He took Chrissy from her and strapped both children into their car seats. What else could he do but slip his arm around her and hold her close. She dropped her head on his chest and shuddered, as if trying not to cry.

"It's okay," he whispered, pressing his cheek on her silky hair, rocking her slightly as he would a little child. "Nothing happened. You just got a scare."

She stayed where she was a moment longer, then slowly pulled away. Brody released her reluctantly, then gave in to an impulse and gently brushed her tears from her cheek with the knuckle of his forefinger.

"I'm sorry," she said, swiping her hand over her cheeks. "I feel like such a wreck."

"You don't look like a wreck at all," he said, fingering a strand of hair away from her face. "But your car isn't going anywhere tonight."

She sniffed again, looking back at her vehicle illuminated by the headlights of his truck. The back tire was flat and Brody was sure the "clunk" she said she heard would make the car undrivable.

"I'll check out the kids and see if they're okay," he said.

Not for the first time Brody was thankful for his EMT training as a firefighter.

But a quick check of the children, smiling and safely strapped in their car seats, showed him they were fine. He wasn't surprised. The car had simply driven off the road.

He took Chrissy out, handed her to Hannah, then took Corey out and stepped away from the car. "You go sit in the truck with the kids," Brody said. "I'll move the car seats. We'll get you home."

She nodded and pulled in a quavering breath. He paused, just a moment, watching her make her way up the side of the ditch, a slight figure carrying two babies silhouetted against the lights of his truck.

She looked so alone it hurt his heart.

He shook off the feeling and pulled open the back door of the car, hoping he could figure out how to get the seats out. It took some fiddling and muttering and a few bumps of his head on the roof of the compact car, but ten minutes later he had the seats fastened in the back of the truck.

"I just remembered, my purse and diaper bag are still in the front of the car," Hannah said.

"I'll get them. Anything else?"

She shook her head.

So while Hannah clipped the kids in, he returned to the car to get what she'd asked for. He found the purse and bag on the floor of the front passenger seat, and as he pulled them out, he caught the glint of metal swinging from the rearview mirror. He paused, looking at David Douglas's dog tags. A potent reminder of Hannah's past.

Was he crazy to think he had a chance with her?

He returned to the truck and gave Hannah the diaper bag and purse and got into his side. "What about the car?" she asked.

"My dad and I will take care of it. And you're positive you're okay?" he asked again, needing the assurance.

"Yeah. Just shook up. I'm so thankful nothing happened to the twins." He could see her profile in the lights from the dashboard. Though she clung to the diaper bag, her chin was up and she looked as if she was pulling herself together.

"When we get back to Jasper Gulch, I'll call my dad," Brody said. "And we'll make arrangements to get your car towed to town."

"I'll have to find a way to get the twins after work—"

"You don't worry about that. My mother can bring them back to town for you, too. Or I can. It will get taken care of."

"I can figure something out," she said. "I might be able to borrow a vehicle from my parents."

"Don't worry about it. My mother is only too happy to help you out. She has often said how much she admires you and how you've gotten through all you've had to deal with."

"Lots of panicky prayers," Hannah said. "And lots of help from my parents. I couldn't have managed that time after David's death without them."

His mind ticked back to the dog tags still hanging from her rearview mirror. He didn't want to bring David into the moment, but he felt he had to ask. He sensed things were shifting between them and he didn't think he imagined those moments of connection. He couldn't be that obtuse or hopeful that he imagined it all.

"Do you still miss him?"

Hannah's silence made him feel like smacking himself on the head. She had just had a traumatic experience and now he was going to bring up her dead husband whose dog tags she still had in her car?

"Not as much as I used to," she said quietly. "Sometimes it seems so far away I wonder if being married to him actually happened."

"You weren't married that long."

"Just a couple of months. Obviously long enough to get pregnant," she said with a light laugh that surprised him. "But David was a part of my life for so long."

"You were dating already when my family first moved to Jasper Gulch."

"You remember that?" she asked, sounding surprised.

He squeezed the steering wheel and decided to go for broke. "I remember everything about you when we first moved. You wore your hair in a ponytail and I always wanted to give it a tug whenever you came bopping past me in the hall, wearing a slouchy sweater, long scarf and skinny blue jeans and laughing with Julie Shaw."

She said nothing to that and for the next few moments the only sound in the cab of the truck was the hum of tires on the asphalt and the muted country music coming out of his stereo. In the distance Brody could see the glow of lights from town coming closer.

A few minutes later, they were parked in front of the hardware store. Brody got out and carefully released Corey from the restraints and pulled the warm, sleeping bundle of boy into his arms. Corey moaned, then laid his head on Brody's shoulder.

This felt too good, Brody thought as he followed Hannah, who was carrying Chrissy, up the narrow stairs to her apartment. She unlocked the door with one hand and turned to him. "I can take it from here," she whispered.

"No. Just tell me where to put him." His mother, thinking ahead, had bathed the kids and put their sleepers on so they were ready for bed.

"Follow me," Hannah said, leading the way, the light above the stove in the kitchen casting a wan glow through the apartment. She carefully opened a door just off the living area. The room, illuminated by a bear-shaped night-light, was small and packed. Most of the floor space was taken up by two cribs and a change table. But nothing was out of place, he noticed.

Brody laid Corey in his crib and then covered him with the blanket that hung over the side. Corey pulled the blanket over his shoulders and emitted a sigh of deep satisfaction.

Hannah stroked Chrissy's cheek, bent over and kissed her, then Brody moved out of the way so she could do the same with Corey.

He walked out of the room and she followed him, carefully closing the door behind her.

"I think they're out for the night," she whispered, releasing a slow sigh, smiling at him, the muted light in the apartment casting her face into intriguing shadows.

Brody slipped his hands into the back pockets of his jeans. It was the only way he could stop himself from reaching out to her again.

"That's good," he said. "And about your car. Like I said, my dad and I will take care of it. We'll bring it into Gary Finney's mechanic shop to get fixed up."

"Good to know." Then, to his surprise, she took a

step closer to him. "I can't thank you enough for coming to get me. I was so relieved to see your lights down the highway."

"Alfie was there," he said, taking a stab at humor to deflect his own emotions.

"He was the other reason I was relieved to see you," she said, her smile deepening.

"I'm glad I could help."

She released a light laugh. "You know, I feel bad now. I didn't trust you with Corey on that horse, yet I counted on you to help when me and the kids were in trouble. I'm sorry about that. I should have trusted you."

"It's okay. I understand," he said. She looked up at him again, and Brody, once again, went for broke. He laid his hands on her shoulders, waited a moment as if she was a nervous filly he was ready to tame, then he slowly drew her closer, his arms slipping around her slight figure. He looked down at her, gauging her reaction and, when she didn't move, didn't say anything, he lowered his head and pressed his lips to hers.

She melted into him, her arms sliding around his shoulders, her fingers tangling in his hair as she returned his kiss.

And Brody knew, in that moment, everything had changed for them.

"You don't need to do this if you don't want to," Brody said, standing inside the corral, holding the reins of a pinto mare that had the most benign of names. Blossom. The mare was saddled up and stood, head hanging down, eyes half-closed, looking docile. Brody's horse was also saddled up and tied to the fence.

The late-afternoon sun shone warmly on Hannah's

back, but she still felt a chill feather down her spine at the sight of the saddled horses.

This morning, when Gina picked up the twins, she had told her that Brody had a surprise for her back at the ranch when she came. Apparently this was it.

"I wouldn't put you on a horse that would hurt you," Brody assured her. "My sisters rode Blossom for years. She's bombproof. I would trust her with my life. Besides, she's also had twins, rare for a horse. I thought you two might have something to talk about."

He gave her a broad smile that helped his cause. A bit.

"Why are you doing this again?" she asked as she slowly climbed over the rail fence and into the corral.

"Because I can't imagine anyone being afraid of horses, and it bothers me that you are. I think you're missing out."

Hannah wiped suddenly sweaty palms over her pants, then walked over to the horse.

"Just pet her for now," Brody said. "Get used to her and let her get used to you."

The sharp scent of horse mingled with old leather and rope brought back a quick stab of fear, but Hannah fought it down and reached out and petted Blossom.

The mare opened her eyes and lazily turned her head as if checking Hannah out.

"We're going to be best friends, right?" Hannah said, stroking her carefully, the horse's rough mane tickling the back of her hand.

"She likes you," Brody said. "I can see it in her eyes. You okay to get on now?"

"That was a pretty brief introduction," Hannah said.

He just smiled again, his one hand holding the reins as he held his other hand out to help her. She took it, but just before he was about to help her on, he bent over and brushed a quick kiss over her lips.

For some reason, that kiss rocked her more than the one they had shared last night. This kiss was like the kiss of two people comfortable with each other. Trouble was, *comfortable* was not a word Hannah could use around Brody. He made her feel confused, alive, energized and excited. Not comfortable.

"Okay. I'm ready to get on," she said, feeling a need to create a bit of space from which she could examine the situation better.

Last night, after he left, she had lain in bed, staring up at the ceiling, reliving their shared kiss again and again. It had shifted the ground beneath her feet. Thrown her off balance.

But at the same time it had created a feeling of rightness.

It was all too confusing and right now, sitting on the back of a horse seemed like an easier task than analyzing her changing feelings for Brody Harcourt.

Brody looped the reins over Blossom's head and handed them to her. "Hang on to these and the pommel of the saddle at the same time, put your foot in the stirrup, lean ahead to get your center of balance and swing your leg over her back as you get on."

"Like in the Westerns," she said with a shaky laugh.

"Sure," Brody said.

She pulled in another breath just as Blossom blew, signaling her impatience. Then Hannah did what Brody told her and put her foot into the stirrup to get on. It wasn't the most elegant of mounts. Her leg caught the back of the saddle and she fell forward, but she recovered and managed to get her other foot in the stirrup.

"Looks like the length is good." Brody ducked under

the horse's head to check her other foot. "We're good to go. You ready?"

Hannah gripped the reins so tightly she thought she was going to lose all feeling in her hands, and gave Brody a curt nod.

"Just hold the reins loosely," Brody told her as he picked up a rope attached to the halter Blossom still wore. "And release that tension in your shoulders."

Hannah didn't even realize she had her shoulders hunched up until Brody pointed it out. She rotated them, trying to loosen them. She wished she didn't feel so uptight. She wanted to be all cool and casual and confident.

She wanted Brody to be proud of her.

"We'll just make a few laps around the pen so you feel comfortable," he said. "Anytime you want to stop, just let me know, okay? You're in charge here."

"That's something I haven't felt for a while," Hannah managed to joke.

"That's the beauty of riding. You are always the one in charge. You're the one who tells the horse when to stop and when to go."

Blossom started, then gave a little stumble, which sent Hannah's heart into her throat. But then the horse recovered and soon they were keeping an easy pace. Hannah kept her gaze fixed on Brody's broad shoulders as he walked ahead of her, turning now and again to give her an encouraging smile.

As they made a few more rounds, she found herself relaxing, letting the rhythm of the horse's plodding hooves reassure her.

"You're doing great." Brody's approval made her feel more confident as they walked for a few more minutes. "Now I'd like you to make her stop by pulling on the reins," Brody said. "But don't jerk. Just a gentle pull back until you feel some resistance."

Hannah nodded and slowly drew the reins toward her, pleased when Blossom stopped at the faint pull. They repeated the exercise and after that, Brody got her turning the horse first one way, then the other. All the while he walked alongside her, encouraging her and correcting.

But with each command, each new thing she tried, Hannah was surprised to feel her fear easing away. "Do you want to try on your own while I ride beside you?" Brody asked.

Hannah looked down at him and as she looked into his eyes, she felt a desire to show him that yes, she could do this. That something that he enjoyed so much she could try to share with him.

"Yeah. We can do that."

So they spent what was left of the daylight walking the horses side by side around the corral, stopping, going, turning and twisting. And each time Blossom responded to the faint movements of the reins, Hannah felt her confidence growing.

Then Winston came to join them, leaning on the top railing of the fence, his hat tipped back as he watched. "Way to go, girl. Very brave of you."

She gave him a thankful smile, then suddenly realized how late it had gotten. "The kids—"

"Are fine. Gina just told me to come and get you for supper."

"We'll be there in about ten," Brody responded. He turned back to Hannah. "You okay to quit? I don't want you to get too sore."

"Yeah. That'd be good."

He dismounted, then helped her off Blossom. "Just

stay here. I'll unsaddle and unbridle the horses and bring them out to the pasture."

She nodded, crossing her arms against the cooling air, watching as he worked, his movements quick and efficient. He talked to the horses while he worked. The horses stood quietly for him, and in no time the saddles were returned to the shed just off the barn. He brought the horses to the pasture and then returned, his casual grin creating an answering warmth.

"Hey, there," he said, his voice growing quiet as he stopped in front of her.

"Hey, yourself," she returned, her voice growing breathless. "Thanks so much for giving me that. For making me try something that scared me."

"I hope you're okay with it?" he asked. "I didn't want to push you, but I really wanted you to experience how enjoyable riding can be."

"And why would you want that?" she asked, unable to suppress her slightly flirtatious tone.

He gave her a crooked grin, as if he knew what game she was playing. "I don't know. I thought, maybe, you and I could take the horses out on a longer ride. If you're ready."

"I might be. With more practice."

"That, I can give you." Then he ran his finger lightly up and down her neck, sending delightful shivers dancing down her spine. "So, you're okay?"

She sensed his question held more than a mere inquiry after the state of her nerves. She let the thought settle, giving it proper weight. Then she returned his smile, laid her hand on his shoulder and stood on tiptoe to brush a kiss over his cheek. It was rough, faintly whiskered, but the contact created a quiver of happiness.

"I'm just fine," she said.

"As for the horses, would you be interested in an easy ride tomorrow? Dad and I have to ride up to the south pasture to check on the cows."

A picture of herself on the back of a horse, roaming the hills, looking all adventurous as she rode beside Brody, flitted through her mind. Then, with a sigh of regret she shook her head, reality dissipating the daydream. "I have to clean my place up and get caught up on laundry and groceries. All those typical, boring Saturday things that take up so much time."

"Too bad. It would have been fun." He brushed his knuckle over her cheek. "Will I see you Sunday?"

"Yes. I'd like to try church again."

His smile made her even more determined to make the effort. "I think the kids will be okay."

"I think so, too."

"And thanks again for taking me out on the horse," she said quietly. "I was afraid at first, but I'm glad you made me do it."

"So I'm not a bully?"

She laughed at that. "No. Not at all. It was good for me to push myself past my comfort zone. And…" She hesitated a moment, still uncomfortable with baring too much of her soul.

"And what?" he prompted, his hand squeezing her shoulder lightly, encouraging a response.

"And to let myself trust you."

That netted her a moment of silence. Then Brody brushed a kiss over her cheek. "You can always trust me" was his quiet response.

His words settled into her soul and she held them.

When he took her hand and they headed toward the house, brightly lit on the hill, she felt a sense of rightness and homecoming that was both exciting and, if she was honest, a bit disconcerting.

An image of David slid into the periphery of her thoughts and she brushed it aside.

Later, she promised the memory as she and Brody walked, hand in hand, up the walk to his parents' house where her children waited. *I'll think what to do about you later.*

Chapter Eight

❧

"The kids were fine." Janet Hearn handed Corey to Brody, then picked Chrissy up and gave her to Hannah. "They didn't cry at all."

"I'm so glad," Hannah said, taking her diaper bag from Janet. Though she had been assured that the nursery staff was more than capable of taking care of the twins if they fussed, and though Gina had often commented on how happy they were when they were at the ranch, Hannah still had a hard time leaving them in the nursery. All through the church service she kept expecting to be called out to deal with them. It made it difficult to concentrate on Pastor Ethan's sermon, but she could have easily blamed Brody's presence beside her for that same distraction.

"Do you need a ride to your parents' place?" Brody asked as he settled Corey on his hip.

Hannah regretfully shook her head. "Julie said she and Ryan would bring me." Though Gina had made it clear that Hannah was more than welcome to come to the ranch for Sunday dinner, and though part of her wanted to take Gina up on the offer, Hannah also wanted to visit with her parents.

And to give herself some breathing space from the feelings Brody created. Since that kiss Wednesday night and the days she and Brody had spent together since then, she had felt herself being pulled through a variety of emotions and she wasn't sure how to sort them out.

"And how has your mom been feeling?" Brody asked as he held open the door leading outside.

"Good enough to have me and the kids over. She said she might be ready to take care of the twins again this week," Hannah said, walking down the ramp toward the parking lot.

She wasn't sure how to feel about that, either. Having the kids at the ranch had been amazing. She loved that Gina took them out every day. That they got exercise and fresh air. That they could play with the kittens and have Chance follow them around. It was an idyllic setting. But at the same time, she felt as if things were moving so quickly between her and Brody that maybe some breathing space and stepping back might be a good idea.

"That's too bad," Brody said. "I was getting used to having the munchkins around every day."

She glanced over at him and caught him looking at her. Another one of those moments they seemed to share so frequently the past few days. They walked down the wooden ramp, through the group standing around outside.

"Lots of new faces in church this morning," Brody commented as they worked their way around a knot of chatting people.

"There's been a lot going on in Jasper Gulch." Hannah's diaper bag bumped against a young couple as she made her way through the gathered crowd. "I'm so sorry," she said, pulling the bag closer to her.

"No need to apologize," the young woman said, turning to Hannah. It wasn't hard to see the baby bump under her black-and-white polka-dot dress. "How old is your girl?"

"Thirteen months," Hannah said. "And how far along are you?"

"Not far enough. Seven months. But I'm expecting twins, so I can be excused for my size," she said with a light laugh. "Your children must be twins, too?"

Hannah nodded. "This is Chrissy and that's Corey."

The woman's eyes shifted from Hannah to Brody and she smiled. "They sure look like you," she said to Brody.

Hannah's heart shifted as she shot Brody a glance. But he didn't look fazed by the women's comment. "They do resemble their father," he said, neatly avoiding explanations to someone who didn't need to know.

"Such a lovely family," she said, adding further to Hannah's discomfiture.

"Thank you," Hannah said quietly. "I hope you have a lovely Sunday."

"We will. We plan to take in the fair at the end of the week. Anyhow, you and your husband and kids have a great day," she said.

Hannah mumbled her thanks, then walked away, unable to look over at Brody and equally unable to stop the flush that was now warming her cheeks.

She didn't blame the woman for thinking they were a family. Brody was holding Corey. She was holding Chrissy. They were walking together.

"I'm sorry about that," she said as she dug in her diaper bag for the keys. "That must have made you feel strange."

"Not really. She didn't know." His casual response gave her pause. "Did it bother you?"

He was looking directly at her, but she couldn't read anything from his expression. Then she shook her head. "It was an honest mistake."

And yet, as she watched Brody buckle Corey into the car seat, she caught herself thinking about Brody and family and fatherhood. The twins would never know David as their father. The thought created a feeling of uncertainty braided with sorrow. And yet as Brody straightened, then smiled at her, she couldn't stop a feeling of fullness and promise.

Was she allowed to feel this?

"Looks good," Brody called out to Dylan as he held his hand up. Brake lights flashed, the lumbering fire truck rolled to a halt and Dylan jumped out of the cab.

"We should get a lot of traffic in this spot," Dylan said as he walked toward Brody, glancing at the setup. "Who did you have to flirt with to get this space?"

Brody grinned as he pulled open the back door of the truck's cab. "Hannah did this without any input from me."

"Speaking of, here comes the lovely Hannah herself," Dylan said, winking at his friend.

Brody couldn't stop the quick lift of his heart.

Sunday night Hannah had called to let them know that her mother was feeling much better and would be taking care of the twins again. Brody's disappointment surprised him. While he knew he would be seeing Hannah again, he also knew he would miss the kids. They were so cute and fun to have around. His mother had been mopey the past few days, and Brody could tell she was worried, as well. He wanted to console her, tell her that things seemed to be shifting between him and Hannah, but he wanted to be sure himself before he said anything to either of his parents.

There were days their expectations pushed at him, making him feel an extra tension around Hannah.

So it was probably just as well that when he saw her the past few days, it was without his parents hovering. Watching. Longing.

Yesterday he and Hannah had met at Great Gulch Grub for lunch; today they had arranged to meet at the fairgrounds.

"Hello, Dylan. Brody," Hannah said as she stopped close to the booth. The wind was teasing her hair, tossing it around her face.

"Looking good," she said, pointing her clipboard at the truck. "I'm sure the kids will be all over that."

"We hope so. Too bad the twins are too young to fully appreciate it," Brody said.

"Maybe in the future," Hannah said quietly.

Another small promise.

"Brody loves kids, you know," Dylan said loudly, as if Hannah might need reassuring.

"I know he does." Hannah's eyes twinkled, and Brody was glad to see that Dylan's comment amused instead of bothered her.

Brody shot Dylan a knowing look and at first he looked puzzled, then he seemed to catch on. "I…uh… should check the cab. Of the truck," Dylan said, making a big deal of pointing back to the truck. "Make sure we've got the books and hats and suckers and stuff." He then beat a diplomatic retreat.

Brody turned back to Hannah and smiled down at her, a feeling of rightness settling in his soul. "So. How was your morning?"

"Busy. I received some last-minute applicants for

booths that I had to turn down." Hannah shrugged. "I hate doing that."

They were quiet a moment, as if each trying to find their way around this new place they had come to. Finally, Brody broke the silence. "I was wondering if you were interested in heading over to Salem. There's a good movie playing. Could you get a babysitter?"

"Julie might help me out," she said so quickly Brody was reassured.

"I could come and pick you up."

"Great. That'd be great."

He wanted to give her another kiss, but this was too public a place. And Julie was only a couple of tables over and he could see her watching them both like one of her own ewes would an innocent lamb.

"I…I should go and…and check with some of the other participants."

Brody nodded, but as she walked away he felt it. A sense of homecoming. That the boundaries of his life had fallen into pleasant places, as the Bible said.

Then he turned and came face-to-face with Julie Shaw.

She had a big smile on her face, but he could tell that she came on serious business.

"What can I do for you, Julie?" he asked.

Julie looked at him and then shot a meaningful glance at her friend, who stood by another table, scribbling something on her clipboard.

"She's a great girl," Julie said by way of introduction. Julie's blue eyes were enhanced by the color of her sweater, a sky blue that made her auburn curls even redder.

"I think we both agree on that," Brody said, dropping his hands on his hips as if to give extra stability against whatever Julie might have to say.

"Be careful with her. She's lost so much and she doesn't have a lot of reserves." Julie folded her arms over her chest in a defensive gesture.

"What you're saying isn't something I didn't think of," he said quietly. "And I respect that, but you need to know that I would never do anything to hurt her."

Julie seemed to weigh his words. "Sometimes you guys can hurt without knowing you do it."

"I've cared for Hannah ever since I first moved here," he said, wishing he didn't sound so defensive. "But she was always David's girl and I respected that. Still do."

Julie's expression softened and Brody sensed that he had scored a few points with Hannah's good friend. "I'm glad to know that."

"I also think she's stronger than you might think," Brody said.

Julie seemed to consider his comment, then as he and Julie exchanged cautious smiles, he sensed that he had gained an ally in Hannah's friend.

"Hey. Brody. Just got a call," Dylan called out from the cab of the truck. "Fire close to the Shaw ranch. We'll need to take this truck."

Brody shot Julie an apologetic look. "Gotta go," he said and jogged over to the truck, jumped in. In seconds they were rolling out of the fairgrounds, sirens blazing, and leaving behind a group of surprised residents.

"I thought for sure the hero was going to give up on his brother." Hannah stirred a spoonful of sugar into her coffee and set her spoon on the table beside it. "I was getting myself ready for an unhappy ending to the movie."

"I'm glad it ended the way it did," Brody said forcefully. "I hate sad endings."

Hannah took a sip of her coffee, looking at him over the edge of her cup, unable to stop a grin at his vehemence, a feeling of utter contentment washing over her. They had just come from the movie, and when Brody suggested they go for a cup of coffee, she had quickly accepted. She wasn't ready to go back to Jasper Gulch. She was enjoying this sense of time out of time. Just her and Brody sitting in a café in Salem where no one knew who they were, the low lighting and quiet ambience creating a feeling of intimacy.

When she told Julie about the date, wondering who she should get to babysit, her friend had immediately volunteered.

"Did your emergency call this afternoon have a sad ending?" All evening the question had been hovering, waiting to be voiced. Brody hadn't said anything about it, and local gossip, via Rusty Zidek, was that it was just a grass fire most likely set by a prankster. That set her mind at ease, but it was still a call, and when she'd heard the wail of the sirens leaving the fairgrounds, her heart had jumped.

"No. We caught it on time. Though we suspect that whoever set it was hoping it would move into one of the stockpiles of hay the Shaw ranch has situated over its spread. We aren't usually this busy," Brody said.

"Three fires in two months?"

"I think someone is up to something," Brody said. "But we keep stopping them, so no harm, no foul."

He sounded so casual about it all and Hannah wished she could feel the same. Thankfully, this last one wasn't anything major, which put her at ease.

"And how is Finney coming along with your car?" he asked.

"He said it would be ready Friday, so I'm going to walk over and pick it up."

"That's the first evening of the fair, isn't it?"

Hannah couldn't stop a flitter of panic at the thought. So much to do yet. "It is. But that's the only day I could pick it up. I have to make my basket that afternoon, as well."

"And? What are you going to put in yours?"

Hannah heard the leading question in his voice and angled her head to one side, toying with her hair. "It's supposed to be a secret who makes which basket."

"Supposedly. I know that last year the Shoemaker girls made it fairly clear which ones theirs were. They got bid up pretty high."

"I'm sure they'll be up to their usual shenanigans," Hannah said.

"So how will I know which one is yours?"

"You're going to bid on mine?" she asked, unable to keep the coy note out of her voice, surprising herself with her flirtatious attitude.

It's fun, she thought. *I never did this with David. Never had that teasing courtship.*

"You bet I am. I don't want to end up with Rosemary Middleton's or Chauncey Hardman's. She's no lover of cowboys."

Hannah chuckled, imagining Brody sitting with a very chatty Rosemary or a taciturn Chauncey. "Maybe I'll put a pink bow on mine," she suggested.

Brody laughed and then reached across the table and covered her hand with his, toying with her fingers. "Maybe you'd better be more specific."

Hannah released a light sigh as she twined her fingers around his, enjoying this give-and-take. The flirting, the coy glances. The hesitant dance of, what she assumed, was courtship. She and David had dated so long it was as if their relationship had settled into such a familiar place; she couldn't remember this fluttering of her heart, or the way her breath seemed caught in her throat.

Just a look from Brody, just a simple touch, created myriad emotions that were both exhilarating and hinted at possibilities.

"I'll let you know," she said quietly.

"How are the kids doing? I miss seeing them."

Those four words gave weight to those possibilities. "I think they miss being on the ranch. Corey was fussing the other day and all he could say was 'Kitty. Please. Kitty. Please.' It was so adorable." Hannah took a one-handed sip of her coffee and when she set it down, her phone buzzed. She freed her other hand from Brody's and picked up the phone, turning it over. Then she released a gentle sigh when she saw who was calling.

"Who is it? Julie?"

"No. It's David's parents," she said, biting her lip, debating whether she should answer it or not. She waited another moment, then dropped her phone into her purse, stifling her guilt. "I'm sure they're just checking in. I think they came back from their cruise yesterday."

She didn't want to think about Mr. and Mrs. Douglas. After Allison Douglas had given her the package of letters she had sent to David, Hannah had put them in a dresser drawer and hadn't looked at them since. Which, of course, made her feel guilty. As if she was abandoning David and his memory.

She shook the feeling off, but a tiny remnant of it lingered.

But, later that evening, when Brody dropped her off and walked her up to her apartment and kissed her good-night, thoughts of David were erased from her mind.

Julie was reading a magazine when Hannah let herself into the apartment. As soon as Hannah closed the door, Julie got up, her eyes wide with anticipation. "So. How did it go?"

Hannah resisted the urge to touch her lips as if anchoring Brody's kiss.

"It went good, but I'm tired," she said. She gave her friend a benevolent smile. Right now, she wasn't ready to do a postmortem of her date with Brody. Right now, all she wanted to do was go to bed and hold the moments she had spent with Brody close. To savor them alone.

"Sure. Of course."

Hannah sensed Julie's disappointment, remembering all too well the moments she had spent with Julie discussing her relationship with Ryan and the advice Hannah had given her.

But right now, she didn't want anyone giving her advice. Reminding her of her responsibilities. Right now, she just wanted to be Hannah, Brody Harcourt's girlfriend. Not Hannah Douglas, widow of David Douglas and mother of his twins.

Chapter Nine

"Wheel bearings were shot, too," Gary Finney said, wiping his hands on a greasy rag that he stuffed into the back of his blue mechanic coveralls. His balding head was streaked with black, as was the perpetual stubble shading his chin. "So I fixed them, as well."

Hannah could almost hear the flutter of dollar bills leaving her wallet. "And what did that cost?" She ignored the layer of greasy dust on the dented metal table Gary used as a desk for his auto-parts business.

The mechanic part of his enterprise was a small bay in the back of the store. Gary only did auto-mechanic work part-time and, it seemed, only for certain people in town. Though he was related, by way of his grandmother, to the Massey family, he preferred not to let people know that. The Masseys were the other founding family of Jasper Gulch, but Gary always said he was the kind of guy to make it on his own and not trade in on the family's heritage.

Gary shot her an annoyed glance as he handed her the keys. "I'm not charging the widow of the town's local hero."

David again.

"You're running a business," she said, pulling the wallet out of her purse. "I can pay for what you did."

Gary held up a grease-stained hand, his bushy eyebrows glowering over his dark eyes, creating a map of annoyed wrinkles. "You're not going to pay me. I wouldn't feel right. David was a good man."

He was, Hannah thought, biting back a sigh. But there were times she wished that David would be laid to rest. Yes, she missed him, but she was moving on.

Hannah ignored Gary's protests and pulled out her checkbook. "Please, tell me how much I owe you."

"You can write that check, but I'll just rip it up," Gary said gruffly.

Hannah knew when she was beat, but she wasn't going down without a fight. "Okay. I'll let you do this on one condition. You come to the fair tomorrow and bid on a picnic basket and I'll pay for that." They had already received so many baskets Hannah was getting nervous that they might not have enough bidders.

Gary shot her an annoyed frown. "I don't know about that."

"If you don't come, I'll be here every day writing you another check. Or dropping dollar bills off on this counter." Hannah doubted that Gary cared that said bills would probably be well coated with grease.

This netted her another harrumph, which she chose to interpret as reluctant acceptance. "I'll come, but I pay for my own basket, missy."

"We'll talk about that later. So we'll be seeing you tomorrow night?" She stopped herself from adding a suggestion to clean up and shave. If he showed up, that would be good enough for her.

"I said I'll come," he grumbled.

She picked up the keys and got in her car. Her day

had been a flurry of last-minute activity, reminders to women to bring their completed themed baskets to Abigail so she could store them until the fair. The food ones would be coming the day of the fair. She had hoped to display all of them on a table on the bandstand the day of the fair to create anticipation.

She had spent the rest of the day at the fairgrounds, running interference for the participants, fielding requests for last-minute items. Mayor Shaw wanted her to do some work just before she closed for the night, and Robin and Olivia had needed some information for the town history they were putting together. She had promised her mother she'd be at the apartment to have lunch with her and the twins, but things became too hectic, so she wasn't able to.

Now she was done for the day and on her way to Pastor Ethan's. He had come by the office this afternoon, looking extremely sheepish, saying that his words of bravado to Brody had come back to haunt him. He wasn't sure what to put in the basket.

Since Hannah had to make her own basket anyhow, she told him she would help. Her mother had offered to watch the kids a few extra hours, so it all worked out.

She had already picked up what she needed. Her dear mother, bless her heart, had baked muffins and cookies and squares. All she had to add were wraps and fruit that would stay good until tomorrow. And just to be on the safe side, she had doubled up on some items in case Pastor Ethan needed to fill his, as well.

She walked up the sidewalk to the parsonage, a small white house with brown trim. Welcoming and friendly.

"Come in," she heard from the depths of the house.

The door opened and Hannah had to grin.

Ethan wore a large, flour-dusted apron that covered

him from neck to knees, no small feat for a man as tall as he was. His hands were also coated with flour, and some had made it into his brown hair. Hannah also caught a whiff of something burning.

"Hey. Am I glad to see you!" Ethan stood aside, gesturing for her to come in. "Whoever coined the phrase 'easy as pie' needs to check the ninth commandment. It's the biggest fib cloaked in three simple words."

Hannah chuckled as she followed him into the kitchen off the side of the entrance.

"Oh, no. There it goes again." Ethan rushed to the oven and yanked it open, smoke billowing out. The smoke detector started screeching and Ethan snatched a towel and waved it vigorously below the detector.

Hannah slipped on the oven mitts lying on the counter and quickly yanked the overflowing pie out of the oven, then cast about as to where to set it down, the ear-piercing noise of the detector taking over any available thinking space.

But there was nowhere to put the pie. The counter was strewn with remnants of pie dough and filling. A bag of cookies lay on its side beside a bag of bread and a package of cold cuts. Flour dusted most every surface.

So she set the pie on top of the stove and closed the oven door.

Finally the wailing of the detector quit. Ethan tossed the towel aside and dropped into a nearby chair. "This is a disaster of biblical proportions," he exclaimed.

Pastor Ethan might be forgiven a bit of hyperbole, Hannah thought as she straightened the bag of cookies and brushed the leftover pieces of piecrust into a pile. "Do you have a cloth I can wipe the counter with?" she asked, running water into the sink.

He told her where and in a few minutes they had the counter cleaned off to create a working space.

"That already looks more promising," Ethan said, heaving out a sigh. He poked a finger at the pie, which had fallen in, the crust black on one side and a dark brown on the other, its contents still bubbling away through the slits he had made. "This, however, doesn't."

"I don't think we can salvage it," Hannah agreed. "But I brought extra supplies along. I have to do my basket, as well."

"I guess this is what I get for bragging to Brody the other day that baking isn't unmanly."

"It isn't," Hannah said, grinning as he picked up the pie and tipped it into the garbage can at the end of the counter. "But maybe it's just not your gift."

"Obviously not." He wiped his hands on the front of his apron and watched as Hannah set the grocery bags on the table. "So, what are you doing for your basket?"

"My mother graciously did some baking and I bought some other supplies at Middleton's. The baskets, I bought in Salem last time I was there. I didn't want anyone to recognize them."

"So what are we putting in them?"

"I had originally thought of doing a strictly food basket, but knowing that today is the only time I have to do it made me rethink the contents and switch to nonperishables. That way, I can give the finished baskets to Abigail and that's off my mind."

"Sounds good to me," Ethan said.

"So I thought we could use my mother's baking and add some chocolate, candy bars and these cookies."

"But I thought the point was that whoever gets the other person's basket has to eat the food with the person."

"That's how it used to be done, but the logistics of trying to auction off fifty baskets of food seemed too difficult. So I asked half of the people to make themed baskets, the rest food baskets."

"And if the buyer doesn't get a food basket?"

"I was concerned about that, but the midway is selling hot dogs, hamburgers, corn dogs and funnel cakes, so I'm guessing anyone who doesn't get a food basket won't walk away hungry."

"Sounds like you've got it all covered."

"I hope so, though I'm a bit sad it won't be a traditional basket auction like the olden days." Hannah had spent a lot of time trying to make this work so that there wouldn't be a huge rush of food baskets that would be sitting around too long, but it meant making a few sacrifices where authenticity was concerned.

"And who do you hope bids on your basket?" Ethan asked as he set the two baskets on the table.

Hannah wished her cheeks didn't flame the way they did, and though she ducked her head to hide it, she caught a faint gleam in Ethan's eyes that told her he had caught her lapse.

"Lucky Brody," he said quietly.

Hannah pulled out the container of muffins her mother had made. "These need to be wrapped in cellophane," she said, pushing the box of plastic wrap across the table.

"Your mother is feeling better?" Ethan said, his question more of a statement as they tidied up the kitchen.

"Yes. She's taking care of the kids now. Though I have to say I liked seeing them at the ranch with the Harcourts. They sure enjoyed having the kids."

"And I noticed on Sunday that Brody seems fairly comfortable with your children."

Hannah felt warmth flood her cheeks again, and she knew she might as well bring up one of the reasons she had come here. "Yes. He is." She looked down at the cookies she had taken out, rearranging them, fussing with them while she sorted out what she wanted to say. "He seems fond of them, as well."

Ethan wrapped up a muffin and set it aside. "Somehow, though, I sense some hesitation."

She tore off another piece of wrap, then gave up and looked over at him. "I don't know what I should feel. I don't know what I should do."

"What do you mean, what you should feel?"

Hannah blew out a sigh and dropped into the chair behind her. Ethan did the same, resting one elbow on the table, leaning closer, creating a sense of listening and waiting.

"I really care for him." She caught herself there, knowing that *care* was too small a word to encapsulate the feelings Brody created in her. Feelings that, at times, seemed stronger than the ones she ever felt for David. "It's just I have my kids to think about and I feel like David is still so present... Just before I came here, Gary Finney wouldn't let me pay for my car repairs because I'm the widow of a hero. People keep telling me how bad they feel that David died and what a great guy he was, which he was," she hastened to add. "I feel like a fraud because I feel guilty about caring for someone else when everyone else seems to want to keep me pegged as David's widow. Like that's who I am. I mean, sure, he and I were together for ages, but I want to be able to let go at some point and I feel like everywhere I turn, David comes back. And I feel guilty because I am ready to move on and I feel like people aren't letting me."

"I can understand that," Ethan said. "You don't want that to be your identity. And in a small town it becomes hard to move past the memories, the expectations and even the nicknames. People in a small town know every aspect of your life and, at times, feel like they have a vested interest in what is going on in your life. They remember everything about you and, I suspect, for many people in this town they remember how long you and David were a couple."

"I think a lot of people still see me as that freckle-faced girl with the frizzy hair who followed David everywhere he went. Plus, I have Allison and Sam Douglas in my life. I feel like they would never approve of someone like Brody, or anyone. Allison has made it no secret that she would be happiest if I stayed single and never married again."

"You don't need David's mother's approval for what you do," Ethan said quietly. "You need to make the best choice for you and for your children. But just to give her some leeway, she might be concerned that if you date and marry again, and she knows that someone as wonderful as you would, she probably wonders how much the twins would be a part of their life."

Hannah let the idea rest in her mind and, with a sudden flash of insight, realized he was right.

"You might want to assure her of that," Ethan encouraged.

"If I ever date again," Hannah said, picking at a hangnail.

"What about Brody?"

Hannah sighed. "I care for Brody so much that it scares me. I feel like what I felt for David was a teenage love for a teenage boy and I never really grew past that. I probably shouldn't have married him." She waited for Ethan to look surprised. To express some type of shock that she still married David in spite of how she felt, but he just sat there, watching her, waiting. Some of the tension that had gripped her neck loosened at his unjudgmental attitude. "But I can't just think about me. Like you said, I have my children to consider. I have to put their needs above mine. And they need a mother and a father. And that's where I get nervous."

"About Brody?"

She nodded. "I know he's not the Book-it Brody he once was, but sometimes I still sense that he's a bit of a risk-taker. He has a dangerous job. Just yesterday, I was at the fairgrounds and he got called out to a fire. It was just a grass fire I found out afterward, probably set by some prankster, but it still bothered me more than it should have to think he was doing dangerous work."

"I can see that would be a consideration. But at the same time, I think many relationships are made or broken by trust."

She frowned, not certain where he was going.

"Brody Harcourt is a good man. A careful man. Yes, at times in his life, he liked to take risks, but I think you can trust that if he has you and your children in his life he won't take needless risks."

Hannah thought of what he'd said, still not sure what to think.

"We all live risky lives. Every time we get into our vehicle we take a risk. Even just walking down the street can be a risk." He paused there a moment, a shadow flickering over his face. But it left so quickly, Hannah wondered if she had imagined it. "Every time we open our hearts, we take a risk. Anyhow, what I'm trying to say is that our lives are always fragile. You know that firsthand and I'm sure that's why you feel you need to be extra cautious with your own children."

And her own heart, Hannah thought.

"I think you need to realize that God is with you every step of the way in your life," Ethan continued. "That the comfort He gives you isn't some cozy, comfortable feeling, but it is true comfort. That He is always with us. That no matter what we go through, He is alongside us. You could choose to live a life of safety and guard your heart at all times and save yourself the pain of losing someone. You'd spend the rest of your life alone. Or you could take a risk and let someone into your life and know that your life will be the richer for it."

Hannah weighed his words, still uncertain. She had so hoped that talking to Ethan would help her make a decision. Instead, she felt more confused than before.

"Just listen to your heart," Ethan said. "I know it sounds corny, but I think there's merit in paying attention to your emotions, as well. But now, enough advice from me," Ethan said, slapping his hands on his thighs as he stood and looked over the table scattered with foodstuffs. "Why don't you tell me what we need to do next."

"Ah, memories," Brody said as he inhaled a deep whiff of air laced with deep frying and food cooking. All around them they heard squeals and laughter, punctuated by the tinny music of the carousel and the other two rides on the midway. He pushed the twins' stroller over the uneven grass of the fairgrounds. He was walking alongside Hannah, who was inspecting the booths, her clipboard clasped in one hand, cell phone in the other.

Though the fair wasn't officially open until tomorrow, the midway had opened up at four o'clock this afternoon. This made setting up more difficult for those exhibitors who were putting finishing touches on their displays, but at the same time it created an expectant energy for tomorrow, when the fair would go all day. He and Dylan had finished work on their booth this afternoon, and a couple of the other guys were there now, stocking up on plastic fireman hats, coloring books, crayons and other freebies the kids might need. Tomorrow he would take turns with the other volunteers to man the booth and show kids the truck.

He just hoped they didn't get a call again. For some reason, there had been a spate of vandalism lately and he wished that Deputy Calloway would get to the bottom of it.

"You know, some of my favorite memories are of eating corn dogs and finishing that off with funnel cakes," Brody said, giving the stroller another push over yet another bump. "I should get you one of each." He turned to Hannah, who walked slowly alongside him, staring at her phone. "Uh-oh. You've got your town-hall-secretary face on," he said.

Hannah's frown deepened as she looked at him, then she laughed. "I'm sorry. I just got a message from Abigail that she and Chauncey Hardman just moved all the baskets from her house to a shed. I need to call her about that."

She tapped out a number on her phone and then stopped, phone pressed to one ear, her hand to the other, clipboard clamped under her arm. "So where did you move them?" Brody heard her ask. "Are you sure it can be locked? Can someone keep an eye on them, because I'm just not comfortable with the baskets being there."

From the sound of her voice and the way she was biting at her lip, Brody could see she wasn't happy with this particular turn of events. "I wish you would have run this past me," she said. "But I guess it's too late to change all that now." She nodded as she listened some more, then said goodbye. When she was done, her eyes were snapping with a frustration that surprised Brody. Other than the afternoon when she'd found him with Corey on the back of the horse, she was usually calm and self-possessed.

"That Abigail. Honestly," she huffed as she clutched her phone. "I don't know why she didn't run this by me."

"So why did she move the baskets?"

"She had been storing them at her place and got tired of them being there, so without letting me know, she moved the baskets to one of the sheds in that clump of buildings on the edge of the fairgrounds."

"The old Shoemaker homestead?"

"Yes."

"One of those buildings does have a door that locks, as far as I can remember. Mr. Shoemaker's old toolshed apparently. They should be okay there."

Hannah sighed and massaged her forehead. "I hope so."

"I doubt that baskets with books, bath beads and baby stuff will have much value to a thief," Brody said, taking a chance to steal a quick kiss.

Hannah chuckled as she straightened. "I guess you're right. And the rest of the baskets will be coming tomorrow."

"Is your basket in there?" Brody asked, trying to sound all casual.

"Probably. Pastor Ethan said he would drop it off at Abigail's." Then she stopped, pressing her fingers to her mouth as if to catch back the words she had just said. "You weren't supposed to know that."

"So I just need to know what kind of basket Pastor Ethan brought and I should be good to go," Brody said, stroking his chin, pretending to plot. "Though I could end up with Ethan's basket if I don't play my cards right."

"And whoever might want to bid on Pastor Ethan's might end up with mine." Hannah put her hand on Brody's arm. "But seriously, you can't tell anyone that he's making a basket. He wanted it to be a secret. He just wants people to know that it was made by a man."

Brody waved his hand in front of his face. "Lips. Sealed."

She laughed, which made Brody smile, which created that curious feeling of well-being that had been sifting into his life more often. And especially when he was around Hannah.

Corey burbled his pleasure at the sights and sounds of the carousel turning beside them, red, blue and yellow horses bobbing and cars sliding by, all accompanied by the ubiquitous bouncy organ music that made him smile.

Chrissy joined in, reaching her chubby arms out as if asking if she could go on.

Brody looked from the carousel to the kids, then to Hannah. "What do you think? Would they be okay to ride if we stood beside them?"

Hannah hesitated, then glanced at her phone.

Brody sighed, then gently pried the phone from her hand and dropped it in his shirt pocket. "You are now officially off duty. It's five-thirty and your kids need to have their first ride on a carousel."

"But—"

Brody placed a finger on her lips. "Let's go. They'll love it."

Hannah sighed, as if releasing the work of the day, then nodded. "That would be wonderful."

A few minutes later, they stood beside each other, Chrissy supported by Hannah as she sat on one red, white and blue horse, Brody beside her holding Corey perched on a flame-red horse with gold sparkles. The twins rocked back and forth, clinging to the single poles holding up the horses.

"I think they want to get going," Brody said, steadying Corey as he leaned too far forward, his hand slipping on the pole.

"They sure are excited." Hannah grinned at Brody and then lurched as the carousel started going, the music playing louder as it gained speed. The horses bobbed, the music sang, and as they circled, Brody kept his hands on Corey, but his eyes stayed on Hannah, standing right beside him.

She was laughing, looking as carefree as her kids. She glanced over at him and her smile shifted. Grew deeper. Softer.

"Thanks so much for this," she said quietly. Then, still supporting Chrissy, she leaned forward, caught him by the neck with one hand and pressed a kiss to his lips.

"Why, Hannah Douglas, stealing kisses on the carousel," Brody said with mock seriousness. "You are a forward miss."

"I'm learning," she said with a lift of one eyebrow. Then to her surprise, he returned her kiss with one of his own.

"Brody. Brody," Corey babbled, leaning toward Brody.

Hannah pulled back, her startled gaze darting from her son to Brody.

"Did he just say what I thought he said?" Brody asked.

"I think he did," Hannah said, laughing, albeit a bit nervously. Did she have a problem with this?

"Brody. Brody," Corey repeated clearly, leaving them with no doubt at all.

"That's…amazing?" Brody looked at Hannah with a measure of confusion. Was this right? That this little boy was saying his name? At the same time, he felt a twist in his soul. It felt right.

"Are you okay?" Hannah asked.

Brody laughed, then kissed Hannah again. "I'm more than okay. Are you?"

"I'm great," she said.

Then Chrissy laughed, slapping the pole, and Hannah joined her. And as they spun around and around, the four of them together, Brody knew this moment, with this woman and these children, was what he wanted for the rest of his life.

He hooked one arm around Hannah, holding her close, his other arm around Corey. He wanted to tell her now, but knew this wasn't the time or place.

Soon, though, he promised himself. Soon he would let her know how he felt and hope and pray she felt the same.

Chapter Ten

"I've got to get these kids back home and to bed," Hannah said as she caught Chrissy rubbing tired eyes with a sticky hand. Corey scratched at his ears and then yawned. They were both back in their stroller and Hannah and Brody were sitting on a couple of folding chairs by the fireman's booth.

Though the midway would be here tomorrow night yet, Brody had insisted on giving the twins the full fair experience tonight, reminding her that tomorrow she would be busy with the auction and myriad other things.

So she gave in and let herself enjoy the fun of having Brody win her and the twins some cheap stuffed animals, buy them way too many mini doughnuts and corn dogs and share an oversize bag of neon-pink cotton candy.

Half of which was now spread over Chrissy's and Corey's faces.

"I'll come with you," Brody said.

"That would be nice." She tried not to sound coy, but felt a flush of pleasure at his offer.

They got up and walked across the bumpy ground and back to the parking lot, navigating their way through crowds of laughing people, acknowledging some waves and hellos.

Julie and Faith were laughing at Cord and Ryan, who were trying to shoot down some bottles at one booth. Hannah could see Robin Frazier wandering around, looking bemused as she took in the busyness. Rusty Zidek had come for a while, but Hannah couldn't find him, though his camo Mule was still parked at the edge of the fairgrounds.

She had hoped to corral Abigail Rose, but she hadn't seen her tonight. She was still upset that the woman had moved the baskets without asking for her input, but on the other hand, it wasn't Hannah's apartment that was getting taken over by the things.

"You look worried," Brody said, slipping his arm over her shoulders again.

He did that with such ease, such a sense of familiarity, that Hannah felt a deep settling in her soul.

"I was thinking about those baskets. Silly, I realize, but I know how much work some people put into them and I'd hate to see anything happen to them."

"I'm sure they'll be okay."

"If someone is willing to steal the time capsule, who knows what else they might be tempted to steal?" Hannah said, feeling a sudden flicker of premonition.

"I still think there is more to this time capsule than simply theft. I wonder if someone doesn't have something to hide."

"If that was the case, then why didn't it get unearthed sooner?"

"My job is simply to speculate about the issue. Not resolve it," Brody said with a laugh. "So, where did you park?"

Hannah looked around, momentarily disoriented in

the gathering dusk. Finally she saw her vehicle. A few minutes later, they had the kids stowed in the car and were on their way, Hannah driving.

Brody was tapping his fingers on the dash of her car, looking suddenly solemn.

"What's on your mind?" she asked, giving him a poke to get his attention.

He pulled himself away from wherever he had been and grinned at her. "Nothing."

"Guys always say that," she grumped as she drove into the parking lot behind the hardware store and turned off her car. "But I don't believe that."

"Well, it's true," he said, getting out and opening the back door. "You know there's a ton of boxes in a guy's mind. Work box. Friend box. Food box. And then there's the nothing box. When I'm working, I've got the work box open. When I'm eating, the food box. And once in a while, I like to go to the nothing box and just look at it and think about…nothing. Don't you have a nothing box?"

Hannah laughed again as she unbuckled Chrissy. "I might. Who knows? I have not had the luxury of spending any time there if I did. Kids, work, food and sleep have been my main priorities for the past year and a bit." She realized that had the potential of sounding whiny. "Not that I mind, you realize," she hastened to add.

"I know you don't mind," he said quietly. "I know you love your kids. Anyone can clearly see that. Even when they're as grubby as they are."

"Thanks to you," she returned as she dug her keys out of her diaper bag.

"Hey. You're never too young to get sick on food from the fair."

Hannah laughed again, surprised at how at ease she

felt. Though she had a million things to do and organize yet, this moment of time she had spent with Brody and her kids had created in her a sense of possibility.

For the first time since David's death, she felt expectation and, as she watched Brody, walking ahead of her up the stairs leading to the back door of her apartment, a sense of attachment that was much, much stronger than friendship.

"So, bath first?" Brody asked as they stepped inside the apartment and he flicked on the lights.

"For sure." Hannah tossed her keys on the table just inside the door.

"You get their pj's. I'll start running the bath."

Hannah was about to protest, but a look from Brody stopped that. "Okay. I'll do that," she agreed.

Twenty minutes and four gallons of splashed water later, Hannah was toweling Corey off while Brody was wrestling with a squirming Chrissy, trying to get her arms stuffed into her sleeper.

"Are you sure this thing is the right size?" he asked as he tried once again.

"It might be a bit small," Hannah admitted sheepishly. "They've grown a bunch the past couple of months, but I haven't had time to get them new clothes. And Middleton's doesn't carry baby clothes, so I have to wait until I get to Bozeman again." She stopped there, realizing that she was sounding too apologetic.

"I've got to go to Bozeman for tack next Saturday. We can pick up some stuff then."

He said it so casually, as if it was an automatic assumption that she would come along with him.

She tested that thought a moment, stealing a quick glance at Brody, who was finally zipping up the sleeper, looking proud of his accomplishment.

Was that where they were headed?

Did she dare go there? Was she ready? Could she do this?

At that moment, he looked over at her and she felt as though she was back on the carousel, turning and spinning, but having Brody beside her centered her. Made her feel as if she was in a solid place.

Tell him, a small voice urged. *Let him know how you feel.*

Did she dare? Because she knew once she let herself go down this path, there would be no turning back.

Ethan's advice came back to her.

You could choose to live a life of safety and guard your heart... Or you could take a risk and let someone into your life...

She took a breath, sent up a prayer for strength and courage and was about to speak, when Brody's phone rang. It sounded like a fire alarm.

He jumped to his feet, yanked it out of his pocket and immediately answered the call. His voice was brisk. Staccato. No nonsense. Then he hung up and shot her an apologetic look. "Sorry. Gotta bail. There's a fire at the fairgrounds. I left my truck there, can I borrow your car?"

Her heart turned over in her chest as she also hurried to her feet and grabbed the keys from the table where she had thrown them when they came inside. She gave them to him; he gave her a tight smile, a quick kiss.

"Be careful," she said, fear winding like a snake around her stomach.

She had said these exact same words to David when she said goodbye to him.

"I will. I'll call you when I'm done. It's probably just

another grass fire. Don't worry." He kissed her again
and then he was gone.

Don't worry, he'd said.

Easier said than done.

She put the twins to bed, trying not to rush, trying
to quell the panic that licked, like hungry flames, at
her soul.

"Mama, Mama," Chrissy called out, reaching out
to her as if afraid.

"Just go to sleep, honey," Hannah said, smoothing the
still-damp curls away from her daughter's face. "Have
sweet dreams and may God watch over you."

And Brody, she added.

Chrissy stuck her thumb in her mouth, turned over
onto her side and her eyelids drifted shut.

Corey was already breathing heavily, lying on his
back, his arms flung out as if he was still flying on the
carousel.

Hannah tucked their blankets around them, tiptoed
out of the room and carefully closed the door.

Then she hurried over to the window overlooking
Main Street, her heart leaping into her throat when she
saw the orange glow above the roofs of the buildings
across the street. Panic seized her with an icy fist and,
try as she might, she couldn't loosen its grip.

She pressed her chilled hands together, knuckles
turning white as she clutched them under her chin.

"Please, Lord," she prayed. "Please, Lord."

She wanted to rush out of the house, to run down the
street and find out what was going on. But she had to
stay here, waiting, wondering, worrying.

Just as she had when David shipped out.

It will be okay. It's not as dangerous.

She tried to listen to the quiet voice, but the fear

and panic leapfrogged over it, slamming forefront in her thoughts. She wanted to phone her mother but was afraid to get her worrying, as well. Instead, she picked up her phone and dialed Julie's number but was sent directly to voice mail. There was no way she was leaving a message, so she ended the call.

She turned away from the window and walked to her bedroom, dropping onto her bed. Her Bible lay there. Buoyed by the worship services, inspired by Pastor Ethan's message, she had started reading it again.

Moments later it lay open on her lap as she flipped through the pages. She didn't know what she was looking for, but she needed something. She found Psalms and began reading, seeking, looking, feeling like a wanderer through the desert, seeking even the smallest drop of water.

And then she remembered Psalm 46. Her father used to read it often, whenever her mother would start down her worry road, as he called it.

Her fingers flew through the pages and then, there it was. She took a deep breath and started reading aloud.

"God is our refuge and strength. An ever present help in trouble. Therefore we will not fear though the earth give way and the mountains fall into the heart of the sea." She read more slowly, letting the words soothe her fears, wrap themselves around her stuttering heart. She came to the end and read, "The Lord Almighty is with us. The God of Jacob is our fortress."

Her softly spoken words echoed a moment in the silence of her room and she lowered her face in her hands, not sure what to do, what to think, how to pray. Her mind whirled back to those moments when she opened the door of this very apartment and saw the uniformed army officials.

I can't do this again, she thought, rocking back and forth, her arms wrapped around her middle, trying, struggling to find peace.

Because, deep in her heart, she knew that though losing David was hard, losing Brody would be harder.

Hannah jumped to her feet and returned to the window, unable to keep from watching the glow above the roofs, peering into the night, unable to keep the panic from circling her mind like angry crows.

"I think we got it all." Brody leaned on the shovel he had been wielding and looked around the blackened trees, checking for the slightest sign of smoke. The sun was slowly coming up, adding much-needed illumination to the glaring lights of the trucks and flashlights wielded by the volunteers and the Jasper Gulch firefighters.

He blinked as another rivulet of sweat seeped past his soaked helmet band and into his eyes, but he saw neither glowing embers nor wisps of smoke.

One of the firefighters from the Forest Service was on his knees in full gear, plunging his bare hand into the dirt, moving it around, then repeating the action. Finally he sat back on his heels and pushed up his visor. "This was the last hot spot and it's cold."

Brody pulled off his gloves and wiped yet another rivulet of sweat from his face. They had spent the past eight hours fighting the fire that had started in the Shoemaker buildings, then, as the fire spread, trying to contain the flames that started in the trees.

It had been a long, grueling night, and Brody felt as if he couldn't lift his foot one more step.

Captain Daniels trudged toward them, looking as

worn as Brody felt, his yellow coat and pants liberally streaked with soot.

"What's the verdict, Corrigan?" he asked the young man on his knees, who stood, using his Pulaski to stand.

"Nothing here. It's cold."

The chief nodded. "This was the last trouble spot. Newton and Sawchuk are doing one more sweep," he said, wiping his face with a paper towel, handing the roll to Brody. "But I think we can declare it out."

Brody took the towels, ripped a couple off and handed the roll to Lance Corrigan, the young man from the Forest Service.

"Good job, guys," Captain Daniels said, giving them both a curt nod and then walking on to the rest of the crew, made up of Jasper Gulch firefighters, volunteers and a crew from the Forest Service, to spread the news.

Brody looked over his shoulder at the remnants of the buildings that had, a few hours ago, been an inferno of flames and smoke. All that was left were the concrete foundations of two of the three buildings, a few blackened timbers that now leaned drunkenly against a collapsed tin roof, and the blackened hulk of what, he suspected, had been a cast-iron woodstove.

How was he going to tell Hannah that the baskets were now bits of ash? He couldn't even tell which building was the one they had been in, not that it mattered. Anything inside had been completely torched.

Dylan straggled over, tugged off his sooty helmet and tucked it under his arm. "I'm headed for a shower and then bed. What about you?"

"I should call Hannah, but it's early yet."

Dylan shrugged. "She's got two little kids. I doubt she sleeps in much. It's six-thirty. If she's not awake now, she will be soon."

"You're probably right," Brody agreed, rolling his neck to ease out the kinks. Now that the fire was officially out, he felt the weariness that had dogged at him finally take over. He stifled a yawn and followed Dylan to the fire truck, tugging his own helmet off. He wanted to take his heavy fireman's coat and pants off, but he couldn't until he got the order. He got to the truck, set his helmet under his seat and just as he reached for his jacket, his cell phone rang.

Surprised that it still had juice, he picked it up and glanced at the screen. Hannah.

"Hey, girl," he said, letting a slow smile slip over his face. "You're up early."

"Are you okay? Nothing happened?"

"No. I'm okay."

"Why didn't you call me?"

He frowned at the shrill note in her voice. She sounded scared. "I just got off the fire a few minutes ago."

Silence followed that comment.

"Hey, are you okay?" he asked. "You don't sound too good."

"I'm not."

Those two words sent a splinter of fear through him. "I want to come over."

"No. It's okay."

The tension in her voice made him think it wasn't.

"Give me about half an hour and I'm coming over. We need to roll up hoses yet." He could grab a quick shower at the fire station—he was sure he had a change of clothes there. Then he could walk across to her place.

"I'll see you later, then," she said, but there was no warmth in her tone. Just a cold statement.

Brody said goodbye, then ended the call and tossed

his phone onto the seat of the truck. He couldn't stop a premonition curling around his midsection.

"You don't look too good," Dylan said, dropping his hat back on his head. Until they were completely done, it was full gear.

"I've got to go see Hannah. She sounded all weird."

"You go. I'll cover for you."

"You sure?"

"Go. Now."

Brody didn't need any more urging. Hannah's cold, detached tone gave his exhausted feet wings and, ten minutes earlier than he said he would arrive, he was knocking on the door of her apartment, running his hands through his still-damp hair.

The door was yanked open and Hannah stood in front of him, her hair pulled back in a tangled ponytail, her face looking haggard and worn. She looked more tired than he felt. He wanted to give her a hug, but as he moved toward her, she stood aside to let him in.

The apartment was quiet. Obviously the twins, tired from their outing last night, still slept.

Brody turned to Hannah, who had closed the door and was leaning against it, keeping her distance.

"So you're okay?" she asked, that same distant tone in her voice.

"Yeah. I'm fine. I would have called you but we were going flat out all night."

Hannah's only response was a long, slow intake of breath.

"I can't do this," she said, her tone flat. Unemotional. "I can't live with this 'not knowing.' This fear. Last night I was so scared." Her voice broke. Brody made a move toward her, but she held her hand up to stop him. "I can't do this again."

Her words were like a cleaver. "What are you saying?" He hardly dared ask. What he wanted to do now, more than anything, was to take her in his arms. To hold her close and tell her that he wasn't reckless. That he was careful.

But the look on her face kept him rooted to where he stood.

"I think you need to leave, Brody. Now."

"Okay. I get that you need some space."

She shook her head so quickly strands of her hair came loose from her ponytail. "No. Not space. I need you to leave and not come back."

He swallowed, wishing, praying she didn't mean what she said. Then she stood aside and opened the door with a finality that sent ice through his veins. "Please, go."

He hesitated, hoping it was just her overheated emotions speaking, trying to make eye contact, but she wouldn't look at him.

So he swallowed whatever it was he wanted to say, and without another look at the woman who held his heart in her slender hands, he left.

Chapter Eleven

"The fair will go on," Mayor Shaw said, standing by Hannah's desk, his arms folded over his chest. "Thankfully, the fire was far enough away from the booths and the midway that nothing besides the picnic baskets got damaged."

Which was more than enough for Hannah.

"I got a few calls from some booth participants wondering about that, so I'll call them back," Hannah said. "The midway people were also concerned, so I'll call them, as well."

Hannah massaged her temples, wishing the pounding would go away. She'd had no sleep last night and, in a desperate need to keep busy, she had called her mother to see if she could come earlier to watch the twins. As soon as her mother showed up, Hannah had come across the street and opened the office, diving directly into her work.

The image of Brody standing in front of her, his expression desolate, haunted her all morning and she couldn't shake it off.

Nor could she shake off the feeling that she had made a colossal mistake. But what else could she do? She couldn't live a life of fear. She couldn't live with the reality that something could happen to him.

Her heart felt as if it folded in her chest at that thought. Losing David had been hard. Heart-wrenching, even.

However, last night, even the thought that something could happen to Brody dived deeper than the pain she felt when David died. So much of her sorrow for David was wrapped up in the fact that he would never see his children. She had lost David and had survived.

But the thought of losing Brody seemed to shake the very foundations of her life. She couldn't live with that fear every day.

"We need to carry on and I need to talk to Captain Daniels and find out if he knows what happened," Mayor Shaw was saying, dragging his hands over his face.

Hannah pulled herself out of her troubles, concerned about the haggard look on Mayor Shaw's face.

"Are you okay?" Hannah asked. "Things seem to be piling up on your shoulders, as well."

"I'm fine. Just frustrated with what's been going on in our town the past few months. This anniversary was supposed to be a highlight. A time of celebration, but it seems to have brought out the worst in some of our citizens." He sighed again, then gave Hannah a tight smile. "For now, though the fair will go on, I am wondering if we shouldn't cancel this picnic basket auction."

"Not all the donations were brought in last night," Hannah said, thinking of the meager number of people willing to make food baskets today. "We could still have it with what is donated today."

"Will it be enough?" Mayor Shaw asked. "I know we had talked about fifty baskets."

Hannah glanced over at the papers she had pulled together—the names of people who had already donated baskets that were now soot and ash—and felt overwhelmed. Even under ordinary circumstances, the workload would be stressful.

But now, after the stress of last night and breaking up with Brody this morning, it seemed insurmountable.

You're the one who told him to leave. Don't complain if it hurts.

However, it did. More than she thought possible.

You didn't have to send him away.

"I think it's better than nothing," she said, pulling her attention to the task at hand. "We can't have a fall fair without a picnic basket auction. We simply won't have as many."

"You look tired, as well," Mayor Shaw said, giving her a kindly smile.

Hannah waved off his concern. "Didn't get much sleep last night."

He gave her an absentminded smile, then left. Hannah was about to return to her work, when the door of the town hall opened and Lilibeth Shoemaker walked in, clutching a brightly colored basket wrapped with cellophane and tied at the top with a silver bow.

"Here's my basket. I was going to say sorry it's late, but looks like it's a good thing I didn't bring it yesterday," she said, setting it on the counter.

Hannah nodded, blinking back the pain of her own headache, then turned her attention back to Lilibeth.

"Thanks so much for your contribution," she said, getting up. "We are going to need all the baskets we can get."

"Yeah. I heard that most of the baskets got burned in the fire and that the fire was set on purpose." Lilibeth snapped her gum and crossed her arms over her chest. "I also heard Brody was fighting the fire?" Lilibeth said, concern lacing her voice. "He okay?"

"Yeah. He's fine."

"Good to know."

A wave of weariness washed over Hannah and her mind went blank. Though she needed to keep busy, she felt as if she couldn't deal with one more thing. Part of her just wanted to go home, curl up in bed and push everything away. The same way she felt after David died. But, as she had after David's death, she knew the best thing to do was to keep going.

Besides, David's parents had called and asked if they could take the twins to the fair. Then they had asked if she could join them. She didn't have time, but had agreed, mostly because of what Ethan had said. She wanted to assure them that Corey and Chrissy would always be a part of their lives.

Besides, she had just given up on her one chance to have someone else in her life. What other man would take her in, a woman with two children already and David Douglas's widow?

"I had hoped to have about twenty-five baskets coming in today, but turns out I only have about fifteen, counting yours. That won't be enough."

Lilibeth chewed her gum, thinking. "You know, we could get Vincente at the GGG to help us out. We could make, like, box lunches instead. Wraps, sandwiches. Those are easy to make a bunch of. Get a group of women baking stuff at home and delivering it to the GGG and a few others putting them together there."

Hannah considered the idea. "That could work. It's just they'll all be the same."

"We can make some different, but who cares. I

thought the main idea was that whoever buys the box or basket gets to eat it with the person."

"But if it's a secret—"

"It's never been a big secret," Lilibeth said with a grin. "My sisters always put something on their basket to let whoever they want bidding on it to buy theirs. Just like I'm sure you're going to put something on yours so that Brody bids on it."

"I'm not donating a box or basket," Hannah said, fighting back the ache that the mention of his name created. "Pastor Ethan and I made a couple yesterday but he gave them to Abigail. I'm sure they're burnt up right now."

Besides, she didn't want to make a basket and share it with anyone else but Brody. And she was fairly sure even if she did make one and Brody was at the fair, he wouldn't bid on it. She had made it clear that she didn't want him in her life.

Lilibeth pointed her chin at the stacks of paper that Hannah had sitting on her desk. "Those the people who made baskets?"

"Yes. The ones that got destroyed."

"You give that list to me and I'll get me and my sisters to phone all of them and see if they're willing to do something else."

"I'll talk to Mayor Shaw and see if he'll approve to cover Vincente's costs."

"Okay. Here's my number. Give me yours and we'll stay in touch." Lilibeth pulled out a cell phone and in a matter of seconds their numbers were in each other's phones. "You don't worry about this. It will all come together," Lilibeth said.

Hannah felt a huge load drop off her shoulders at the girl's offer. She handed her the papers, holding on to them for a brief moment. Lilibeth gave her a puzzled look. "What?"

"I'm sorry," Hannah said, releasing her grip. "I'm so sorry that we suspected you of stealing the time capsule."

Lilibeth shuffled the papers, then released a gentle sigh. "That kinda hurt, but I guess if someone sent you a note with my initials…" She shrugged. "I mean, who else could L.S. be? But I'm glad you don't think I did it."

"We doubted from the start that you were the culprit, but we had to follow through on the note," Hannah said with genuine regret.

Lilibeth nodded. "Well, here's my chance to prove Jasper Gulch wrong," she said a gleam of determination in her eyes.

"Thanks again. You have no idea what a load you've taken off my shoulders."

"That's good. And if you have time, stop by the triple G. You can make a new basket for the auction."

"I don't think so."

"Brody will be disappointed," Lilibeth said with a knowing wink.

"Doesn't matter what Brody thinks." Hannah pressed her lips together, fighting down a wave of sorrow.

"Hey. What's wrong?" Lilibeth asked.

Hannah waved her off, forcing herself to smile. "Nothing. It's okay."

"No, it's not. You look upset." Then Lilibeth narrowed her eyes, as if something had just occurred to her. "Did you and Brody have a fight? I mean, it's no secret you two like each other." Lilibeth gave her a coy smile. "I saw you two kissing on the merry-go-round yesterday."

The flush warming Hannah's cheeks was as unwelcome as it was unexpected.

"It w-wasn't really a fight…" Hannah wished her voice wasn't breaking like that.

"But something happened, didn't it?" Lilibeth said, sympathy lacing her voice. "Was it bad?"

Hannah wasn't sure what had gotten into her. The moment, the emotions, the fact that another woman was showing her some sympathy. "Yeah. It's…it's over between us."

The finality of those words seemed to suddenly hit her and she choked back a sob.

Lilibeth put down her papers and, to Hannah's surprise, gave her a tight hug. "I'm so sorry. That's gotta be rough. I mean, for you with your two kids, it's probably hard to find someone."

In spite of her sympathy and Hannah's own wavering emotions, she had to smile at Lilibeth's blunt honesty. "Well, it's because of the two kids that I needed to break up with him."

"You broke up with him?" Lilibeth's incredulity made Hannah, once again, doubt the wisdom of what she had done. "Then I guess it's really over between you two."

Hannah pulled back and tugged a tissue out of the box on her desk. It was running low. She had been using it all morning. "Why do you say that?" she asked, dabbing at her eyes, hoping her mascara wasn't running.

"Brody's not the kind of guy to give a girl a second chance. My sister dated him awhile. She wasn't sure she wanted to stay in Jasper Gulch, so she kind of told him they should take a break, but he said they either move on or they're off. They never dated again. I heard he was seeing a girl in Bozeman after that. Same thing. She broke up with him and then she changed her mind. He said no. They were over. He said Book-it Brody doesn't look back. Got to be kind of a thing with him. He's a proud kind of guy."

Hannah felt as if the breath had been sucked out of her as the reality of what Lilibeth told her hit her.

What did that matter, she told herself, wiping her eyes again. It *was* over between her and Brody. She couldn't live like that. Wondering. Worrying. She had her children to think of.

But even as she tried to tell herself this, other images slipped into her mind. Brody so careful with the kittens, so patient with her on the horse, so cautious with Corey and Chrissy. She tried to brush the thoughts away. It was over. She had made the right decision.

Lilibeth patted her again. "Hey. It's okay. You'll be fine. You seem like a tough lady."

"Thanks, I think," Hannah said with a quavery laugh.

Looking suddenly self-conscious, Lilibeth stepped back and picked up the papers she had set down. "I'll take care of this and you, well, you'll be okay."

"Thanks, Lilibeth," she said, wondering if she would.

"Don't even start that, mister," Brody said to Dylan, who was covering his mouth, stifling a yawn. "You'll get me going."

Dylan just shrugged as he bent over to get another batch of plastic fireman hats for the kids that were stopping by the booth they had set up at the fair.

The smell of smoke from the fire still hung in the air. Even the sharp smells of corn dogs, funnel cakes and mini doughnuts couldn't mask the constant reminder

of what had happened last night and the repercussions
for him this morning.

Brody rubbed his eyes, as if trying to erase what had
happened this morning. The steady, jangling tunes of
the carousel and the electronic bleeps, buzzes and chirps
from the other rides were like a drill in his exhausted
brain. He had to fight his annoyance at the continuous
noise. He knew his feelings had less to do with the noise
of the fair than with what Hannah had told him fewer
than twelve hours ago.

Stop. Move on. Book-it Brody doesn't look back.

But the old mantra, much like the nickname, wasn't
a part of him anymore.

"Can't believe you're not more tired," Dylan said,
handing out a coloring book and some crayons to the
young children that had stopped by their booth. "At
least I grabbed some sleep. You've been going steady."

It was the only way he could keep his mind from reliving what Hannah had told him.

"I'm beat," Brody admitted, fighting another yawn.
"I'll stay a couple hours more, then go home."

"You're not staying for the basket auction?" Dylan
sounded surprised. "But—"

"Hey, kids, want to go into the fire truck?" Brody
asked, cutting his friend off midquestion, walking away
from Dylan to the kids standing in front of their booth.

"Can we? That would be awesome," the oldest boy
said, his eyes wide with amazement. Brody got permis-
sion from the mother, who followed him to the now-
gleaming truck parked behind their booth. It had taken
him and the guys most of the morning to get it back
to parade-ready condition. The tires weren't as clean
as he would have liked and some of the supplies inside
were missing, but for the most part it didn't look as if it

had been involved in fighting a fire fewer than twelve hours before.

He showed the kids the various parts of the truck. Let one sit in the driver's seat, and when they were done, he gave them each a plastic hat and got them to pose in front of the truck where Sawchuk stood with a camera.

"I understand we can buy a copy of the photograph?" the boy's mother asked.

"Just fill in this sheet with your name, address and phone number if you want a print." Brody got the numbers of the pictures from Sawchuk and put them on the sheet, then handed it to the woman. "If you pay us now, we'll mail the photo to you."

He blinked back his own weariness as he watched her fill in the paper, smiling at the little boy who stood at the table, barely able to look above it. In a couple of years that would be Corey.

Would he be around to see him?

And where else would you be?

Brody dragged his hands over his face, as if to erase what had happened this morning and the consequences. Could he truly stay around in Jasper Gulch and see Hannah and her kids regularly?

Another family came by and he helped the kids get their pictures taken, all the while fighting his own weariness. He wanted to get back to the ranch. Leave town behind. Retreat and regroup. Pray. Think. Figure out where he should go from here. Move on, like his dad always told him. Don't look behind you.

Then, as he was helping a little boy out of the fire truck, he heard the familiar laughter of a child. A woman calling out Corey's name. And then—

"Brody. Brody."

Corey?

He spun around, his heart twisting as he saw little Corey toddling toward him, his grin as wide as his outstretched arms as he wobbled and wove over the uneven ground, Sam Douglas right behind the little boy.

"Come back here, you little stinker," Sam said, catching him and picking him up. But Corey leaned away, arms out to Brody, calling out his name. "Brody. Brody."

Then, right behind Sam was Hannah, looking flustered and worried as she hurried to her father-in-law's side. "How did he get away?" Hannah was asking, reaching out for Corey.

"Brody," Corey called out again, in single-minded determination.

Brody looked from the little boy, then over to Hannah. She was watching him, a curious expression on her face.

I need you to leave and not come back.

Those words, uttered with such a sense of finality, reminded him that it was over.

So why was she looking at him?

He looked from her to David's father, who was watching him, his expression puzzled.

Probably wondering why his grandson was calling out his name, Brody thought. Then Allison Douglas joined her husband and the look she gave him was one of polite dismissal.

If ever he needed a reminder that he would never be able to supplant David in Hannah's life, that was it.

He turned away from her, gave Corey a pat on the head, then forced his attention to a group of children who came running toward the booth.

"It's the fire truck place," one of them called out, a young boy of ten with bright red hair and a mouth smeared with cotton candy. "Can we go on it, Mr. Fire-man?"

"Of course you can," Brody said with false hearti-ness. He didn't want Hannah to see how badly she had hurt him.

He brought the kids to the truck, but, unable to stop himself, he shot a quick backward glance over his shoul-der. But she and her in-laws and the twins were gone.

"So what was that about?" Dylan asked him after the kids left.

"They wanted to see the truck," Brody said, delib-erately misunderstanding his question.

"I mean, what was that about with Hannah, doo-fus," Dylan said, cuffing his shoulder with his hand. "I thought you two were, well, dating? You didn't say anything to her. You two acted like each other didn't exist. You have a fight?"

Brody tidied the packages of crayons and straight-ened the coloring books. "It's over."

"What happened?" Dylan insisted.

"You're like a girl," Brody grumped, walking away from him to the truck.

But Dylan followed him inside, watching as Brody fussed with the flashlights, straightened the gear and wiped an infinitesimal spot of dirt from the shining steering wheel. Finally Brody couldn't stand it any-more. He swung down from the truck and turned on his friend, hands on his hips. "I went to see her this morn-ing. After the fire last night. I was barely in her apart-ment when she told me it was over between us. Told me to never come back. Sounds kind of over to me, okay?"

"Did she say why?"

Brody dragged his hand over the back of his head and grabbed at his neck, wishing he could ease away the tightness that had taken residence there. "Said something about being so scared and she couldn't do this again. Said that she couldn't live with the not knowing and the fear."

"Hmmph" was Dylan's comforting response.

"And then she shows up here with David's parents, which is a reminder that I can never live up to this guy. So there you have it," Brody said, pushing past his friend. "And now it's time for me to go home."

"Why? Why home?" Dylan asked, following him.

Brody grabbed his jean jacket from the back of the chair at their table and slipped it on. "Because I'm done here. I'm exhausted and I need my sleep."

"But what about the picnic basket auction?" Dylan asked.

"What?"

"I thought you were going to bid on Hannah's basket?"

Brody just stared at his friend, trying to understand what he was saying. "Are you kidding me? Didn't you hear me say that Hannah doesn't want me around?"

"I heard you tell me about a girl who was scared and who probably overreacted." Dylan handed Brody his cowboy hat. "Maybe she didn't mean it."

"She sounded convincing to me," Brody said, flipping his hat onto his head.

"So you're just going to walk away. Book-it Brody doesn't look back," Dylan said, making quote marks with his fingers and making a face.

"I have my pride."

"And isn't that great company to have in your cabin when you're all alone. You and your television and your dog and your Harcourt pride."

"What is your problem?" Brody glowered at him.

Dylan folded his arms over his chest, his feet planted, looking as if he was getting ready to dress down an incompetent rookie. "You. You and your pride. That's been your problem with Hannah from the beginning."

"What are you talking about?"

"You've always liked her. I know you have. You had a chance when she and David broke up that one summer, but you didn't do anything."

"What could I have done? Swooped in and told her that I'm the one she needs to be with? You're the one who told me that anyone following David would have big shoes to fill."

"What do you mean?"

"That morning we met Hannah at the café a couple of weeks ago and we walked back to the fire station together. I got to hear that story about David and how he got you going back to church."

"I was just telling you that David was a good guy, is all," Dylan protested. "I wasn't telling you to stay away from her."

Brody felt confused.

"See? That stumped look on your face," Dylan said, pointing at him. "It's like you don't think you have anything to offer her. It's like you don't want to fight for her. Like you've always been willing to let David be her guy."

"He was her guy."

"Was. He's gone. You're not." Dylan raised his hands in a gesture of frustration. "Fight for her, man. She pushed you away 'cause she was scared. Show her that you're not giving up on her. Show her that she's worth fighting for. She's probably scared 'cause she doesn't want to lose you like she lost David."

"That's exactly what she said. And how can I convince her otherwise?"

"Just show up. Just be there. Don't give up on her. Swallow your pride and go for her. I've never seen you happier than you've been the past few weeks. I don't think you should just let her go."

Brody looked at his friend, still not convinced.

"Go back to the firehouse or your ranch," Dylan urged. "Take a break. Pray about this and then grab a nap. Come back in a couple of hours and bid on her basket. Let her know you're not letting her go without a fight. It's worth it, isn't it? I mean, what else would you sooner do? Roll over and play dead? That's not the Brody Harcourt I know."

Brody looked at his friend, and, for the first time that day, felt a ray of hope.

And as he drove back to the ranch, he took his friend's third piece of advice and started praying.

Chapter Twelve

The GGG was a hive of activity when Hannah stopped by later that afternoon.

Chauncey Hardman, Jane Franklin and Carrie Landry were busy packaging sandwiches, wraps and baked goods, and from the kitchen Hannah heard more voices of people working. Lilibeth and her sisters were running point, making sure things ran smoothly. Finished boxes were stacked up on a couple of café tables, each box a different size and shape. Young Maggie and Brian Landry were marking them, decorating them with bits of paper and felt markers.

"Hannah, Hannah, a word, please." Vincente Forbes hurried toward her as fast as his portly build allowed, his dark hair even darker with sweat. "I heard you said that the town is paying for the food." He stopped in front of her, huffing as he caught his breath.

"That's right," Hannah told him. "We don't want you to be out for the extra work you're doing."

Vincente pulled back, looking hurt. "I don't want to be paid. I want to donate what I'm doing today. And the food."

"Really," Hannah assured him, "that isn't necessary."

"I'm here to help," Vincente said. "I don't want to be paid. That's my donation to the centennial. I got a lot of extra business from all of this and will be getting a whole lot more. So I want to do this one small thing."

Hannah was touched by his offer. "Thank you so much. That is very generous of you."

"I want this auction that you put so much work into to be a success." He placed his hand on her shoulder. "You're such a brave girl, taking care of those kids by yourself."

Here it comes, she thought. David again, but he simply patted her on the shoulder.

She gave him a quick nod, pleased how she could go through the motions of work, thankful for the busyness that kept her occupied. She didn't feel brave right now. All day she had struggled to keep thoughts of Brody at bay, reminding herself that it was for the best. Better to stop things now, before she got too involved.

But even as that thought formulated, she knew it was already too late. Brody had become so important to her that breaking things off with him now was as painful as anything she had ever experienced with David. More painful, she amended.

When she saw him just a few moments ago at his booth and he turned away from her, she felt a sorrow that had pierced her soul. She kept reminding herself that this was what she wanted. She had done exactly what she knew she should, yet it hurt so, so much.

"We only have a couple more to do," Lilibeth said, joining her. "You sure you don't want to make one?"

"No. I don't," Hannah said. "I think we have enough. Did Pastor Ethan put one together?"

"It's right over there," Lilibeth said, pointing to a large box that was covered with blue tissue paper and decorated with silver stars. "But we should start bringing them to the fairgrounds." She held up an envelope. "I also got the kids to make up name tags that we'll put inside the boxes and baskets so at least our auctioneer, Mick, knows who is bidding on whose basket."

"But how will we get them there?"

"Me and my Mule are at your service." Hannah heard a gravelly voice behind her and laughed when she saw Rusty Zidek standing behind her, his blue eyes twinkling.

And twenty minutes and two trips later, all the finished boxes and baskets were set out on the bandstand, filling up most of the available space. Hannah was arranging the boxes as Lilibeth handed them to her.

"This is amazing," Hannah said, leaning back on her heels to check their handiwork. "After last night, I didn't think this would come together at all."

"Funny how things can change." Lilibeth carried the last box and gave it to her. As Hannah took it, the young girl gave her a sympathetic look. "So, you okay?" she asked.

Hannah wanted to be able to say she was doing fine. Her stock phrase whenever people asked her that after David's death. But this time she only shook her head slowly. "I'll get by," she said quietly, standing up. "I was the one who called it off. I shouldn't be upset about it."

So why did her voice waver like that?

Lilibeth put her hand on her shoulder. "I'm so sorry. I think you and Brody would have made a great couple. He was obviously crazy about you. But then, according to my sisters, he always has been."

"What do you mean?"

"My sister Anabelle was all gaga over Brody when he first moved here," Lilibeth said. "When they started dating, she found out that he kind of liked you. That was one of the reasons she broke up with him. She tried to tell him that you were with David. Always had been and always would be. But Brody only said that sometimes people change and that he was willing to wait and see." Lilibeth gave her a sympathetic smile. "Guess he knows for sure now that it won't happen."

The finality in Lilibeth's voice canceled out the surge of hope Hannah felt when the young girl told her about Brody's ongoing attraction to her.

"Guess not," Hannah said. She felt her heart twist but then glanced over at the boxes, thankful that this, at least, had ended well. "But thanks so much for your help," she told Lilibeth. "You may have not won Miss Jasper Gulch, but I think you've shown your loyalty to the town more than the crowned Miss Jasper Gulch has."

Lilibeth just shrugged off Hannah's praise. Then she looked past Hannah. "Evening, Mayor Shaw," she said.

"Evening, ladies," Mayor Shaw said, doffing his large, black cowboy hat. He glanced over the bandstand and the rows and rows of baskets and boxes. "This looks impressive. You have been busy, Hannah."

"It was Lilibeth's doing," Hannah said, giving the young girl her well-deserved credit. "She was the one who organized the work bee at the GGG. She's been busy all afternoon."

Lilibeth just shrugged off her praise, then beeping from her pocket made her pull out her cell phone. "Gotta run," she said, then turned to Hannah. "You going to be around for the basket auction?"

"I'll see it to the end. Why?"

"Perfect. See ya." And with that she jogged down the steps of the bandstand and was gone.

"So all suspicion has been removed from that young lady," Mayor Shaw said, settling his hands on his hips as he glanced around the busy fairgrounds, as if taking stock.

"Absolutely. She is loyal to the town and has proven herself," Hannah said.

She thought Mayor Shaw would be pleased, but he still looked troubled. "I realize that, but what bothers me is the fire last night. Theft and vandalism are one thing, but that fire could have killed someone. We need to find out who is behind all this, and now that Lilibeth is no longer a suspect, I have an idea who it might be."

"Who do you think it might be?"

"I have an idea, but I don't want to spread any false rumors again. However, I do want to congratulate you on a job well done," he said to Hannah, smiling again. "I'm sure that the auction will raise a goodly amount of money for the town." And with that he was gone again.

Hannah watched him leave, then glanced at her phone. Time to revert to mommy role, she thought, fighting another wave of weariness. Though she had promised Lilibeth she would stay for the auction, part of her just wanted to go home and sleep. Although, she doubted she would be able to do much of that, either.

She shook off her maudlin thoughts. She had to be more like Brody. Keep moving. Look ahead. Don't look back.

It was the only way she was going to get through the next few days. Weeks. Months, even.

Dear Lord, she prayed, *help me get through this. Help me to know that my strength is in You.*

She felt herself waver and leaned against a beam of the bandstand. She stood a moment like that, her head down, waiting for the moment of weakness to pass. She had gotten through this before. She would again.

After a few moments, she straightened and caught herself looking directly at Gina Harcourt, who was watching her, concern etched on her features.

Hannah held her troubled gaze a moment, then turned away. She couldn't deal with Gina right now. She needed space. Space and time. But even as she assured herself, she knew that this time it would be harder.

This time she would be reminded in a physical way, each time she saw Brody, of what she had lost.

"My heart is not proud, Lord, my eyes are not haughty."

Brody leaned back in his recliner and reread the first verse of Psalm 131, trying to put his current life in perspective.

He had been working his way through the Psalms and this particular one was the reading for last night. But he hadn't read it because last night he had been out fighting a fire. So when he had come back from town, he had grabbed his Bible, sat down and turned to where he had last left off, and the words of this psalm had jumped out at him.

You never fought for her. You were too proud, he thought.

As they had all the way to the ranch, Dylan's words circled around the edges of his thoughts. *Show her that she's worth fighting for.* Brody lowered the Bible and let it rest on his lap as he looked off into the middle distance, reliving this morning when Hannah had told him to leave, that she couldn't do this. His first reaction had been frustrated anger. He had just gone through an exhausting fire and instead of being happy that he was okay, she broke up with him.

So he had taken her words and walked away with them.

What else was he supposed to do? She asked him to leave. She pushed him out of her life.

She was emotional. Overwrought.

That much was true, Brody thought. When he saw her face, he was more worried for her than he had ever been for himself.

Swallow your pride and go for her.

He wanted to. So badly. He had cared for Hannah so long and the past few weeks were like the culmination of all that yearning. As if God was rewarding him for his patience. He had given Hannah enough time to mourn and then, when he thought the time was right, he had tried to woo her.

Did he want to give up on all that now?

Brody blew out his breath and got to his feet. Maybe he should go for a ride on Rowdy. Clear his head. He glanced at the clock sitting on the mantel. He had about an hour and a half until the sun went down.

And about thirty minutes until the picnic basket auction.

Please, Lord, I don't know what to do. The prayer was a cry of desperation and confusion. Did he dare go and try to win her back? What if she said no? He would look like a fool. Again.

He paused, trying to decide. Maybe he was making too much of this. So what if he went and bid on her basket and she turned away again? At least he could say he tried. At least he could tell Dylan he had fought for her. And he could tell himself the same. Was his pride more important than the chance that maybe, possibly, she regretted what she had done?

He made a decision and, grabbing his keys, he strode out of his house and got into his truck. A few minutes later, as he was driving down the highway, probably going too fast, his cell phone rang. He hit the receiver for his hands-free unit, staring at the highway ahead, trying to outrun his second thoughts.

"Hey, Brody. Where are you?" his mom's voice demanded.

"I'm on my way to town."

"Good thing."

"Why?"

"I would come down and drag you back here myself. You had better make sure you get here in time for that auction, young man." His mom sounded cranky. "I saw Hannah Douglas standing by the bandstand. That poor girl looked like she'd been kicked by a horse."

His mother's comment made him push a little harder on the accelerator. "What has that got to do with me?"

"I heard from Dylan that she broke up with you."

"Yeah, which means I'm the one who should look like I've been kicked by a horse." He knew he was being contentious, but for some perverse reason he wanted to be reassured that Hannah might have regretted what she had done.

"She's been through a lot. She was probably worried sick when you were out fighting that fire. You need to swallow your pride and give her another chance."

Brody felt a smile tease his lips. "You think I have a chance?"

"You won't know if you don't try."

That didn't sound reassuring, but Brody had to agree with her. He didn't know what would happen, but he also knew that, like his mother and Dylan had said, he had to try.

"Well, I'll be there in about ten minutes."

"You better make it less. They're already starting the auction."

Brody tried to still the panic his mother's words created. He would get there when he got there and in one piece. Even if someone else bought Hannah's basket, he needed to talk to her.

But just to give himself a bit more insurance, he stepped harder on the accelerator.

There was no parking on the fairgrounds and he ended up parking his truck on Massey Street. He had to jog to the fairgrounds, past numerous cars and trucks that filled the grounds. Looked as if there were a lot of strangers here to enjoy the fair. He could hear the sound of Mick's deep voice echoing over the grounds as he called out, "Sold."

Brody doubled his speed, dirt kicking out from his heels, and by the time he came to the bandstand, he saw a few people had already purchased boxes and were finding the owners. Gary Finney stood by Chauncey Hardman holding a box and both of them were laughing. It looked as if Ryan had purchased Julie's, and Mick was announcing another box. Heart pounding with exertion and fear, Brody scanned the crowd but couldn't see Hannah or the twins anywhere.

Were they still here?

He worked his way through the gathering but was stopped by a knot of strangers taking pictures. Ethan stood beside them and gave Brody a quick nod when he joined him.

"So this basket or, shall I say, box, looks like it has been made with lots of love and care," Mick was saying, holding aloft a blue box decorated with gold stars. "I can't say who donated it, but I know that it came from someone very special."

Then Mick looked directly at Brody and his heart hurried up.

"Ten dollars," Brody called out, wanting to get this over and done with.

"I've got ten, do I hear twenty?"

Someone else immediately bid fifteen and Brody was about to bid again, when he felt Ethan catch his arm and lean closer. "You might not want to bid on that one," he said in a low voice as someone else jumped in. "That's mine."

Brody laughed then said, "Thanks for the heads-up." Then he looked at Ethan. "Do you know if Hannah made one?"

"She doesn't know, but Lilibeth and I made one for her."

"Can you let me know when it comes up?"

Ethan gave him a droll look. "You know this is supposed to be a secret."

"And you just told me which one you made."

"Touché. I'll give you a sign," Ethan said.

"Twenty. I have twenty. Do I get twenty-five for this special picnic lunch?" Mick looked over the crowd. "I'd like to add that this box was made by a man, if that makes any difference."

This elicited another flurry of bids. Mick got the box up to forty and was about to call it, when he pointed to Faith Shaw, who was talking to Julie and Ryan, holding her hand in the air as if to indicate how tall something was. "Faith Shaw bids forty and sold."

"What?" Faith called out with a laugh. "I didn't bid on that."

"Oh, yes you did. And this one, I might add, is a very special lunch. Donated by Ethan Johnson."

The crowd clapped, turning to look at Ethan, who was waving and smiling, playing along.

"Looks like Ethan will have to be finding Faith to share his lunch with her," Mick joked. The crowd groaned and then Lilibeth handed Mick another box decorated with pink hearts and stars. Lilibeth scanned the crowd as if looking for someone. Then she caught Brody's eye and she angled her head toward the box just as Ethan dug his elbow in Brody's side.

"This one is Hannah's," he whispered.

Mick glanced over at Lilibeth, who gave him an innocent smile. "Are you helping along the bidders?" he asked with mock severity.

"No. Not at all," she said.

"You Shoemaker girls are famous for getting high bids. Is this how it's done?"

Lilibeth held up her hands as if protesting her innocence, but Mick just chuckled and turned back to the crowd. "Okay, this box has the official Shoemaker endorsement. What am I bid? Let's start at twenty." He easily got twenty, then thirty, then forty.

Brody jumped in at sixty, which caught a few people's attention. In a matter of seconds it was down to him and someone else he didn't recognize. He put in a bid at ninety, a crazy amount for a meal, he told himself, but he wasn't going to lose this. He just hoped Ethan and Lilibeth weren't steering him wrong.

"Ninety-five, do I hear ninety-five?"

Out of the corner of his eye he saw Ethan talking to someone, then pointing to him. He chanced a quick sidelong glance and caught Hannah looking at him, her eyes wide as she looked from him to the box that Mick held up in the air.

You can't avoid me now, Brody thought as Mick called for another bid.

"Going once, going twice—"

"One hundred dollars," a deep voice called out.

Brody swung his head around, looking for this last-minute entrant. Then he shook his head as Cord Shaw gave him a quick salute, as if to say "top that."

Well, he would.

"One hundred and twenty," Brody called back, not waiting for Mick to call out a number.

"One hundred and fifty," Cord drawled, leaning back against the tree behind him, nudging his hat with a knuckle as if to see Brody better.

"Two hundred," Brody returned, looking directly at Cord, daring him to go higher.

"I'm thinking this box is important to you, Harcourt. Why is that? Someone special make it?"

"Bid or quit," Brody said.

"Oh, I'll bid. You're not getting this lunch that easily. Two hundred and fifty."

"Three hundred."

He heard a gasp from beside him and turned to see Hannah. "What are you doing?" Her face held a look of puzzlement, but in her eyes he caught a flare of hope.

"Fighting for you," he said.

"What?"

"Three hundred and fifty," Cord called out.

"Four hundred."

"Keep going, Harcourt, and you'll be spending as much as you would on an engagement ring," Cord said with a smirk.

"That might be coming, too." The words came out before he could stop himself.

He heard Hannah's faint gasp and chuckles from the crowd and felt a tremble of doubt. Then he looked at Hannah and the hope he thought he had seen in her eyes had grown. She was smiling, her hand on her chest.

"Either you really want that bridge fixed or you really like whoever made that box up," Cord said. "Five hundred dollars."

"I'm way beyond *liking* the person who made that lunch," Brody retorted "Six hundred." Brody crossed his arms and settled in as gasps were heard around the gathering, then some whistles and hoots of encouragement. He wasn't sure why Cord was playing this game, but it didn't matter. He was seeing it to the end.

Then nothing from Cord, and as Brody glanced over, he caught Cord's wink and then Brody saw Dylan standing beside Cord and Brody knew exactly who had been egging Cord on.

"Sold to Brody Harcourt. Six hundred dollars," Mick announced with a dramatic wave of his arm.

The crowd applauded with enthusiasm as Mick took the box from Lilibeth. "And the owner of the basket, or box, actually—" Mick opened the box to get the name and for a split second Brody wondered if he had spent an outrageous amount of money on the wrong person. "Hannah Douglas, come up and take your box so you can share it with the winner."

Hannah shot Brody another surprised look, then made her way through the now-applauding crowd. As she walked up the stairs to the bandstand, Brody caught the flush in her cheeks. But when she took the box and came back down the stairs and walked toward him, he also saw the glow of hope in her eyes.

Chapter Thirteen

"Where are the twins?" Brody asked as Hannah led him to a secluded spot under a large cottonwood, a ways away from the gathered crowd. She still couldn't believe he had spent that much on her lunch.

"With my parents and my in-laws, I mean David's parents," she amended. "They're taking them for yet another ride on the carousel. They wanted to treat them and they knew I would be busy with the auction. But Lilibeth said she would take over at the auction, so…" Hannah let her long-winded explanation fade away, feeling suddenly awkward around this surprising man.

"Lucky for me," he said. He stood beside her, shifting his weight, as if unsure what to say and what to do.

Not that Hannah had any idea, either. When she found out that Lilibeth and Ethan had made a lunch on her behalf, she was a little upset. But when she heard Brody bidding on it, her upset had changed to curious hope.

"So, the deal is that you bid on this basket, we get to eat it together. Are you hungry?" she asked.

"Kind of. Haven't been able to eat much today."

"Me neither."

They looked at each other and then Brody finally took the box from her and sat down on the grass.

"Sorry, I don't have a blanket," she said, smoothing her hands over her jeans, then sitting down beside him, unable to quell the anticipation that sang through her.

He held the box a moment, looking at it. Then he looked over at her. "So. Here we are."

She nodded, wishing her heart wasn't beating so erratically. She couldn't breathe properly.

Brody opened the box and carefully peeled back the layer of paper covering the food. "Do you have any idea what's in here? Pastor Ethan said you didn't make it."

"No. The women who were helping Vincente at the GGG did. But I understand that some of the boxes have sandwiches and some have wraps and all of them have some kind of home-baked goodies."

"Wraps it is," Brody said, pulling one out, covered in black-and-white-checked paper. "This one looks like chicken and bacon. Is that okay with you?"

She nodded, taking it. She wanted to say something, anything, but wasn't sure where to start. She wondered if she had imagined his crack to Cord about an engagement ring. She certainly wasn't going to ask him about it. They had other ground to cover.

"I need to tell you—"

"I would like to know—"

They both spoke at once. Both stopped at once, then said, "Go ahead" at the same time, which made them both laugh.

"I'll start," Hannah said, setting her wrap aside and touching Brody's hand as if to create a connection. "I'm sorry I said what I did. I'm sorry I sent you away."

"I'm sorry, too." Brody's long, slow sigh created a dull ache in her heart.

He just bid six hundred dollars for your basket, she reminded herself. *Wait to hear what he has to say.*

"It made for a long, hard day," he continued. He looked over at her and his smile eased away the regret his words caused. "But I'm sorry I didn't stay to talk to you. That I just walked out without looking back."

"You don't go where you're not wanted."

Brody released a cynical laugh, then put his wrap down as well, and caught her hands in his. "I'm a proud, foolish kind of guy. I got told that by a good friend. This morning, when you were so worried and upset, I should have stayed. I should have let you be scared and unload and tell me how you felt." He paused and his words fanned the glimmer of hope she had experienced when he was bidding on her basket. "Then I should have ignored what you said, taken you in my arms and comforted you."

Hannah tightened her hands on his, unable to say anything.

"I should have just held you and told you that I was okay," he continued, his words creating a world where happiness was becoming a possibility. "That nothing happened and that I'm a careful guy and that I would take care of myself because I want to take care of you." Brody fingered her hair away from her face, his eyes holding hers. "I should have fought for you. I shouldn't have let you just push me away."

"I was so scared," she admitted, swallowing down a knot of emotion. "Waiting for you was so hard. I was so worried. I couldn't imagine what I would do if something happened to you, so the easiest thing to do, I thought, was not have you at all."

"I guessed that. And I'm hoping you'll know that

I'm not a risk-taker. I'm not the guy that most people seem to think I am. I'm not Book-it Brody anymore."

"Ethan told me that sometimes people have to leave town to get away from their history and their nickname. You didn't have that chance and neither did I." She pulled in a long breath, stilling her heart, hardly daring to believe that the man she thought she had sent away for good was sitting across from her, looking into her eyes. Holding her hand. Making her feel the blessed possibilities of a future.

"Part of my history that I can't walk away from, and don't want to, is the fact that I've always cared about you. Ever since the first time I saw you."

"But you were in high school. Four years older than me."

"I know. And you were with David." He released a self-deprecating laugh. "But that didn't stop this crazy heart from falling for you."

Hannah could only stare at him as his words seeped backward from this moment to that day she saw him for the first time. She and David had been dating for a couple of years when Brody first moved to Jasper Gulch and yet, when she saw Brody, she felt a traitorous kick of her heart. She had brushed aside her reaction as simply one of a young girl to an attractive man. Now she wondered if, at that moment, she sensed that Brody was exactly the right person for her. Just as she had sensed a feeling of coming home when they started spending more time together.

"I've always cared for you," he said. "And in the past few weeks I've moved beyond that. You need to know that I've fallen in love with you."

Hannah's heart kicked up a notch and as she held his eyes, she felt it again. That sense of homecoming.

That after a long, hard journey she had come to where she should be.

"I love you, too," she said. "And I'm not just saying that because I feel like I should reciprocate. I am saying it because I truly do."

Brody caught her by the back of the head and, drawing her to him, pressed a warm, gentle kiss to her lips. She returned it, slipping her arms around his neck. She couldn't get close enough to this man.

Brody murmured her name and then gently drew back, his dark eyes glowing in the gathering dusk. "You may as well know that I want to marry you."

She wasn't going to cry, she thought, and yet she could feel her eyes fill and her throat thicken. "I want to marry you, too," she managed to choke out.

Brody kissed her again and then sat back. "I didn't think this would ever happen," he said.

"Me neither," she said quietly, catching his free hand in hers and giving him a careful smile. "Especially after what I said to you this morning."

"I know that you were feeling vulnerable when you said what you did," he continued. "You've got your kids to think about and yourself to protect. I get that. And if you want, I'll quit my work as a firefighter. I'll walk away from it."

Hannah could only stare at him. "You would do that?"

"I would. For you and the twins, I would."

She thought of how she had asked David to reconsider when he told her he was enlisting. She felt unpatriotic, but, at the same time, his unyielding stance had made it even harder for them to discuss the issue as a couple. And then, when he insisted they get married as well, she felt as if she had no say in the relationship. No power.

And now Brody was telling her that he would respect her request. If she asked him.

"You are an amazing man, Brody Harcourt."

"You think so?" he said, tilting his head as if to see her from another angle.

"I know so."

"I don't feel like I'm amazing." Brody sighed once, and Hannah sensed that he had something else he needed to say. "I feel like I could never live up to who and what David was. You need to know that."

"You don't need to live up to David," she said, tightening her grip on his hands. "You are who you are. You need to know that I loved him, yes. But the more time I spent with you, the more I realized that what I felt for David was a young, sweet, innocent love. When he left for Afghanistan, truthfully, I felt more sorry for myself than I did for him. I was more selfish then. I didn't really feel married to him."

"What do you mean?" Brody's voice held a tiny edge, and Hannah cupped his handsome face in her hands and brushed her lips over his forehead. Then she lowered her hands and sat back, as if to give herself some distance for what she had to tell him.

"I was having second thoughts about my relationship with David before he enlisted. I just wasn't sure how to express them. What to say and how to say it. David and I had dated for years and years. He was as much a part of my life, it seemed, as my parents were. I had wanted to marry him when I was in high school. Young love and all that. But he wanted to get a stake together. Save up enough so that we could start our lives properly. It seemed the smart thing to do. Just not the most romantic. We even fought about it and broke up one summer over it, but he talked me into coming back to him. So I did. And then he enlisted and I was so confused. Whatever happened to getting our stake? I found out later that he had lost his job and was worried about our future. He thought the army was the best way to provide for us."

She stopped there, feeling a beat of faithlessness telling all of this to Brody. And when he squeezed her hand, she sensed he was telling her it was okay to stop. But she looked up at him, shook her hair back, determined to deal with the shadow of David once and for all.

"I thought this was my chance to break up with him. To give myself some breathing space. David had been such a part of my life, I wasn't sure where love ended and habit took over. I wanted some time to analyze how I truly felt. And then he got called up and he proposed. It was so sudden and so unlike him, I wasn't sure what to do. I wanted to say no, but the thought of sending him off into battle with my no in his ears seemed so harsh. And then, when his parents started in on me, specifically his mother, I felt so railroaded, so pushed, I just went along because it was the easiest thing to do."

She stopped there, realizing how shallow she sounded and how small. "I'm sorry. I'm not as amazing as you have been saying I am," she said, her voice soft.

"Hey. Hey." Brody tipped her chin up with his knuckle, gazing down into her eyes, his dark ones so full of compassion, so full of love, it made her heart turn over. "You *are* an amazing woman. And selfless. I don't know if anyone else would have done any differently in your place."

"It's just been hard with everyone thinking he's a hero, and he is, was, but I feel so guilty when I get these sorrowful looks from people. As if being married to David has granted me some special place in society. I only married him because I couldn't see any other way out. And then I got pregnant." Her voice broke a moment, thinking once again of the anger she felt and right behind it, the guilt that anger always engendered. "I was so upset." She clung to him as if to assure him. "I love my kids. You know I do."

Brody pulled her close, stopped her protests with a kiss. "Everyone knows you do. Hannah, don't be so hard on yourself. All those feelings you've told me about are so normal."

She sniffed and pulled in a slow breath as she laid her head on his shoulder, relishing the protection his arms gave her. The sanctuary. And, even more, the relief of finally releasing what she had held back all this while from her parents and even from her dearest friend, Julie. "I always felt so guilty about it. I felt like I had sullied my marriage vows."

"You said you loved him," Brody assured her. "And you did."

She pulled back and looked at him, tracing his features with her finger. Features of a man who spent his time outside. A man who was a hero in his own right. "I did. But I realized what a shadow that love was compared to how I feel about you." She traced his slow-release smile and returned it with one of her own. "But my other reality is I have two children from that relationship—"

"It's okay, you know," he said, pressing a finger on her lips. "It's okay that David is still a part of your life. That will never change. I love your kids like crazy but I also want them to know what an amazing, heroic guy their father was."

She hesitated again, knowing she had to tell him the rest.

"As well, the Douglases… They are so worried about what would happen if I ever found someone else. We talked this afternoon. I discovered how scared they were that they would lose touch with the twins if I ever got remarried. I want them to stay a part of their lives. I know it creates a complication—"

"They are their grandparents. I know they love them dearly. Of course they will stay a part of the twins' lives."

His words eased away her final doubts and sealed their relationship.

"*You* are an amazing, heroic man, Brody Harcourt," she said. "Not reckless at all."

"Then you'll know I'm not being reckless when I say that I want to marry you. I want to be your husband and I want to be a father to your children. I want them to be my children, too. I want to adopt them. Which, of course, means they'll have a plethora of grandparents. I know my mother and father will be beyond thrilled."

Hannah didn't know whether to laugh or cry. So she did both. Then she kissed Brody again and again.

"How could a day start so lousy and end so perfect?" she said as she finally pulled back, her hands on his neck, her fingers tangling in his hair.

"I thank God it ended the way it did," he said quietly. Then he stood and pulled her to her feet. "We should find your parents and the kids. We need to talk."

He bent over and picked up the box lunch that had sent them down this road. "Are we going to eat this?"

"I've got other things on my mind," Hannah said.

"I don't feel right throwing this away," he said with a wry grin.

"I would hope not, you paid dearly for it."

"More than you will ever know."

"Do you think we can make it to the fairgrounds without anyone seeing us?" Brody asked as he glanced past the tree to the people still milling around the bandstand.

"I doubt it, but we can try," Hannah said, flashing him a smile that seemed to gleam in the gathering dusk.

Brody held Hannah's hand, hoping he wasn't squeezing too hard. He didn't want to let go as they walked away from their secluded spot and toward the fairgrounds. He could still hardly believe this day had ended the way it had. His heart was full. He'd never completely understood the statement until now. He looked down at Hannah, wanting to kiss her again.

As they made their way past the trees, he caught people looking their way and smiling.

"Way to go, Harcourt."

"Congratulations."

"Awesome."

Hannah didn't seem too fazed by the attention, so he decided to accept it, as well.

"Harcourt, wait up."

Brody fought down a beat of frustration as Cord Shaw jogged toward them, grinning. He didn't have time for this. He and Hannah had things to do. He was eager to see the twins again.

And to talk to Hannah's father.

"Well, the best man won," Cord said as he caught up to them. He clapped Brody on the shoulder, then winked at Hannah. "Happy for you two."

"Me, too," Brody returned. "But if you'll excuse us,

I have to have an important conversation with Hannah's parents."

"Of course you do. And after you do that, I want to talk to you about your wedding plans."

"So now you're a wedding coordinator?" Brody couldn't help the gibe.

"Apparently. It's about the Old Tyme wedding we're organizing next month. I'd like you and Hannah to think about getting married then."

"A month?" Brody looked over at Hannah, remembering her comment about feeling pressured to get married to David. "I don't think that's long enough. I don't want Hannah to feel rushed."

Her broad smile showed him he had done the right thing. Then she tucked her arm through his and leaned close to his side. "A month is long enough if it's the right person you're marrying," she said.

Cord looked from Brody to Hannah and it seemed to Brody that a trace of yearning passed over his face. But then Cord smirked, tipped his hat to Hannah and the moment was gone.

"Exactly the right thing to say," Cord said to her. "Call me in the next week if you're interested," he said to them, then turned on his heel and walked away.

"And there goes the world's most hardened bachelor," Brody said.

"Maybe it's because he hasn't met the right person yet," Hannah returned.

Brody looked down at her and smiled. "I just know I have. Now, let's go and find your parents."

Hannah pointed her chin behind him. "Looks like they found us."

Brody turned just as Chrissy and Corey came toddling toward them. "Mama. Brody," they called out.

Brody bent over and caught Chrissy in his arms the same time Hannah bent over and picked up Corey. Hannah's parents hung back, their smiles hopeful and expectant.

But before they joined them, Brody slipped his arm around Hannah's shoulders and hers went around his waist.

"I love you, Hannah," he said quietly. "I'm excited to start our life together. As a family."

She stood on tiptoe and kissed him again, then gave him a smile as bright and wide as the Montana sky. "Family. I like the sound of that."

Then together, they walked over to join her parents.

And make plans for their new life together. Brody, Hannah and their Montana twins.

* * * * *

If you liked this BIG SKY CENTENNIAL *novel,*
watch for the next book,
HIS MONTANA BRIDE *by Brenda Minton,*
available October 2014.

And don't miss a single story
in the BIG SKY CENTENNIAL *miniseries:*

Dear Reader,

This book is about second chances. Second chances for Brody and also for Hannah. Both of them had a second chance at love. Not all of us get that chance. Sometimes life passes us by without the opportunity for a do-over. However, in all the circumstances life brings you, I pray that you may learn, as Hannah and Brody had to learn, that their completeness must first come from God. I know, in my life, I've struggled with thinking that the right circumstances will give me that elusive happiness we seem to chase so hard. Yet all the while I've had to learn that when I rest in God, I find the completeness I'm looking for. Blessings to you as you find your way through your own lives.

Carolyne Aarsen

P.S. I love to hear from my readers. Write to me at caarsen@xplornet.com, and if you want to find out more about me and my writing, visit my website at www.carolyneaarsen.com.

Questions for Discussion

1. Hannah seemed to be initially attracted to Brody but at the same time she held back from that attraction. Why did she fight it?

2. Brody said that he had always been attracted to Hannah. Why do you think he waited until now to pursue her?

3. We never meet David in this story, but he seems to be a very strong presence in Hannah's life. How do you think she felt about the reminders of who he was and what he had done?

4. Hannah and David had dated since they were very young. Have you ever had a "young love"? How do you think that love compared to some of the other relationships you've had?

5. Ethan Douglas told Hannah that sometimes people have to leave town to escape their history and their nickname. Are you part of a small community—whether in a small town, a church community or even circle of friends—all populated with people that have known you all your life? Do you ever feel that you would like a second chance to be someone else somewhere else?

6. When Brody came from the fire to talk to Hannah, she was frightened and worried. How did you feel about her reaction to Brody? Why do you think she sent him away?

7. When I first started this story I portrayed Mrs. Douglas as an aggressive woman who wanted to keep her son's memory alive. But as I wrote, I started to put myself in her shoes and realized that this pressure came out of fear. Fear of losing touch with her grandchildren as the memory of her son—the father of these children—slowly faded away. Why do you think she felt justified in this fear? Are you involved in stepfamilies either as a parent, sibling or grandparent? How do you work around all the expectations and family connections?

8. No relationship is without its problems, even though at the end of this story it seems that Hannah and Brody have solved all of theirs. The reality is that marriage is an ongoing shifting of giving and taking. What are some of the obstacles you think Brody and Hannah will have to overcome in their particular relationship? What could they do at the end of the story that they couldn't at the beginning?

9. Dylan told Brody to "fight" for Hannah. Why do you think he told his friend this? Was he right or wrong? Why?

10. Both Hannah and Brody needed to get to a point in their relationship with God that He became what completed them. Have you ever had to deal with this situation in your life? How did you handle it?

REQUEST YOUR FREE BOOKS!

2 FREE INSPIRATIONAL NOVELS
PLUS 2
FREE
MYSTERY GIFTS

Love Inspired®

YES! Please send me 2 FREE Love Inspired® novels and my 2 FREE mystery gifts (gifts are worth about $10). After receiving them, if I don't wish to receive any more books, I can return the shipping statement marked "cancel." If I don't cancel, I will receive 6 brand-new novels every month and be billed just $4.74 per book in the U.S. or $5.24 per book in Canada. That's a saving of at least 21% off the cover price. It's quite a bargain! Shipping and handling is just 50¢ per book in the U.S. and 75¢ per book in Canada.* I understand that accepting the 2 free books and gifts places me under no obligation to buy anything. I can always return a shipment and cancel at any time. Even if I never buy another book, the two free books and gifts are mine to keep forever.

105/305 IDN F47Y

Name	(PLEASE PRINT)
Address	Apt. #
City	State/Prov.	Zip/Postal Code

Signature (if under 18, a parent or guardian must sign)

Mail to the **Harlequin**® **Reader Service:**
IN U.S.A.: P.O. Box 1867, Buffalo, NY 14240-1867
IN CANADA: P.O. Box 609, Fort Erie, Ontario L2A 5X3

**Are you a subscriber to Love Inspired books
and want to receive the larger-print edition?
Call 1-800-873-8635 or visit www.ReaderService.com.**

* Terms and prices subject to change without notice. Prices do not include applicable taxes. Sales tax applicable in N.Y. Canadian residents will be charged applicable taxes. Offer not valid in Quebec. This offer is limited to one order per household. Not valid for current subscribers to Love Inspired books. All orders subject to credit approval. Credit or debit balances in a customer's account(s) may be offset by any other outstanding balance owed by or to the customer. Please allow 4 to 6 weeks for delivery. Offer available while quantities last.

Your Privacy—The Harlequin® Reader Service is committed to protecting your privacy. Our Privacy Policy is available online at www.ReaderService.com or upon request from the Harlequin Reader Service.

We make a portion of our mailing list available to reputable third parties that offer products we believe may interest you. If you prefer that we not exchange your name with third parties, or if you wish to clarify or modify your communication preferences, please visit us at www.ReaderService.com/consumerschoice or write to us at Harlequin Reader Service Preference Service, P.O. Box 9062, Buffalo, NY 14269. Include your complete name and address.

LI13R

"Bad news," Cord said. "That was the wedding coordinator. She's quitting."

"Ouch. So now what?"

"I'm not sure."

"With no coordinator to help, will you call off the wedding?" Katie asked.

"No." There was too much at stake. The town needed this wedding and the money it would bring in. They had a bridge in need of repairs and a museum they couldn't finish without more funds. "I'll just figure out how to pull off a wedding for fifty couples, maybe get some media attention for Jasper Gulch and hopefully not mess up anyone's life."

"I think you'll do just fine. Remember, it's all about the dress."

"How long are you going to be in town, Katie?" He placed a hand on her back and guided her up the sidewalk.

"I'm not sure. I'm supposed to be helping my sister, but she seems to have escaped and left me here." She sighed and glanced at him.

"Do you think that as long as you're here…"

They were standing in front of the massive wooden doors that led to the church. She had a slightly red nose from the cool morning air and her lips were tinted with pink gloss. As long as she was there, she could be a friend. That wasn't